NEW MEXICO SHOWDOWN

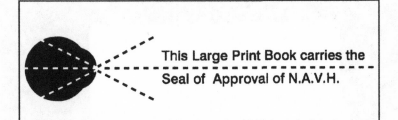

This Large Print Book carries the
Seal of Approval of N.A.V.H.

CHAPTER 1

And then she saw it.

Sitting on the gnarled branch of the dead juniper, the horned owl stared at her, its yellow eyes glowing malevolently.

Dawn felt a flutter in her stomach and knew it was more than the slight shimmy of the child just beginning to bulge her waist. It was fear.

When Dawn was a child in Mexico, before the Apaches came and stole her, and before they changed her name from Maria to Dawn, she had never feared the owl. But the Apaches said the owl flew with the ghost of the deceased and came as a harbinger of death.

But until Sulky took her as his wife, Dawn had doubted them. Sulky was brave, fearing no man. But Sulky feared the owl.

Softly, Dawn began to chant. "Fly away, Owl. Bother another. Go away, Owl. Let the child within me live." Her hands, immersed in a black iron pot, tightened around the deerskin she was tanning in a mixture of brains and water. She glanced alternately from the owl roosting in the dead juniper to the great mountains to the west. There, somewhere in the mountains, Sulky stalked an albino buck. He had seen the buck before and now, he had told Dawn, he wanted its white hide as a robe for his child, the child he knew would be a boy.

Had Sulky not taken her pony to let him graze in the grassy mountain meadows with his own, Dawn would have escaped the owl to find Sulky and safety in the mountains. She wished for a moment that she lived nearer other Apaches on the Mescalero Reservation, not in this remote corner on its eastern boundary. There she might find reassurance among other Apache wives or men. She shivered, knowing they would scorn her even then, because she was Sulky's wife, wife of the man who had led the Blue Coats to the final hideouts of the Chiricahua Apaches, the man who had delivered the severed heads of his own brother and uncle to the White Eyes at Fort Bowie, the man who carried a written note signed by General Crook.

"Go away, Owl, I am a helpless woman," she sang, but still the owl stayed. And stared.

Dawn pulled a hand from the tanning soup and fingered the bearclaw necklace around her neck. Sulky had taken the claws, longer than Dawn's longest finger, from a great grizzly bear. Though mauled badly, Sulky had dispatched the grizzly with his strong hands and a knife. The black claws rattled as Dawn toyed with them and the feathery horns on the owl's head twitched at the noise. The owl must understand, Dawn hoped, that her husband was brave to kill such a large grizzly. And by hand.

She stared to the west, anxious for her husband to come riding over the foothills to protect her. She no longer cared if he came wearing his antlered headdress — sign that he had killed the albino deer — just as long as he returned. And soon.

Never did she remember being so lonely, not even when the Apaches had killed her parents and taken her from Mexico. She fingered the necklace again, pulling her other hand from the chalky soup and shaking it dry. Through her doeskin dress, she patted her stomach, as if reassuring the child that all would be okay, but inside her the child seemed to twist with fear.

"Go away, Owl. We are helpless woman with child," Dawn said softly, but the bird only glared back, its eyes blinking occasionally, its head twisting periodically, its feathers rippling with the sporadic breath of the hot breeze.

Dawn could retreat to the chosa, a primitive cabin of sotol stalks chinked with dirt and rocks and covered with a brush roof, but there was no hiding from the owl. Dare she think of killing the owl? She remembered Sulky's cap and ball pistol, rusty for want of oil and hidden in his brush wickiup on the other side of the chosa. It must be a terrible thing to kill an owl, she thought. For Sulky had killed a grizzly, but never an owl.

"Child within me," she chanted, her fingers still rubbing softly across her stomach, "sing with me to the owl, that he may understand and go away." By the embers of the fire which warmed the tanning solution, she spied a smooth rock the size of a turkey egg. Perhaps she could frighten the owl as much as he had scared her. Slowly, her hand dropped away from her stomach, moving at times no more than the width of a blade of buffalo grass toward the rock. The owl watched, but surely he could not perceive her motive. And finally, after what seemed like enough time for the sun to have risen in the east and hidden behind the mountains to the west, her fingers reached and closed around the still warm rock. Her hand lifted the blackened rock but a hair and Dawn felt a trembling in her arm from the gravity of what she planned.

The owl knew. He spread his wings as if he might fly away. Then he spoke a mournful call, "Hoo, hoo-hoo, hoooo-hoo," and gathered his wings back to his side.

Chills ran down Dawn's spine as cold as the melted snow from the mountain top. The rock, suddenly ice in her fingers, slipped from her hand. Sulky was right. The owl carried spirits that knew her thoughts and understood her terror for herself and her child.

Death must be near, but she could not spot it. She scanned the ground around her for a wicked snake with a rattle on its tail. But it was afternoon and she worked in the heat of direct sunlight. A snake would stay in the shade of a bush until the sun went behind the mountain, but no bushes grew within striking distance. Beyond her work area stood the chosa and beyond that the wickiup. All were in a natural bowl formed by a circle of foothills. The juniper in the center of the depression was rooted at the spot where water seeped from under a pile of rocks that had punched through the tough soil as if they had floated to the

11

surface of the earth. Though not abundant water, it was adequate for two Apaches and their two horses. The depression collected additional water after rains and in the winter it broke the bite of the cold winds swooping down out of the mountains. And, to Sulky's liking, the foothills hid the chosa from the occasional riders who passed this corner of the reservation.

Dawn knew every inch of the ground around her and nothing was amiss. Except the owl.

"Go away, Owl," she sang again and to her surprise, the owl lifted its wings and dropped from the juniper tree, gliding low over the ground toward her. Dawn clutched her throat in terror as the owl finally flapped its wings and ascended the invisible steps in the sky over her head. Its terrible eyes caught hers for an instant. Then the owl was gone, but the image of the owl's round yellow eyes lingered in Dawn's mind and fear fluttered again in her stomach.

And then she saw the riders — four of them atop the foothill opposite where she knelt over the pot with the curing buckskin.

Quickly, Dawn leaped to her feet, flustered from the owl and now from the men. She glanced toward the mountains, but Sulky was nowhere to be seen. Dawn made a tentative step toward the chosa and the four riders nudged their horses toward her. Remembering the cap and ball pistol in Sulky's wickiup, she ran for it instead. Her heart seemed to jump to her throat as she ran and the child within her seemed infected with her terror for he twisted until Dawn feared she might vomit.

At the wickiup, Dawn paused before entering. The wickiup was male domain, Sulky's retreat when she bled between her legs. She glanced over her shoulder. The riders still advanced. Not at a trot, the riders came at a walk, a horrifying pace as if they understood her terror. And enjoyed it.

She burst through the opening into the wickiup, a bare shelter except for the skins on the floor for bedding, his pouch atop it and a few trinkets and clothes from his days as an Army scout. Dawn dropped to her knees on the bedding and grabbed Sulky's pouch. In it, she knew, he kept his amulets, his fire drill, the paper signed by the Blue Coats chief Crook, the secret tokens of a warrior's past, a tiny pouch of arrow poison and the cap and ball pistol said once to have been Geronimo's.

Her hands quivered as she untied the leather thongs around the pouch because Sulky might kill her for opening it. But the

13

riders might slay her if she didn't. She shoved her hand blindly inside, her fingers wrapping around the cool metal of the pistol. Dawn jerked it free and held a revolver for the first time. Its weight sank in her hand, amazing her at how effortlessly she had seen Sulky handle weapons. In his strong hand a weapon became one with his powerful arm, but in hers, the pistol shook like a small leaf in a great wind. The metal was brown with rust, not the shiny gray of the carbine and pistol Sulky had carried into the mountains this morning. Through the opening of the wickiup, Dawn watched the approaching riders. Then she arose and stepped outside to challenge them. Her hand fitted awkwardly around the revolver handle and she tried to lift it, but its weight quivered in her hand. She clasped her other hand on it as well and the revolver was steadier, though still uncomfortable.

Pointing the revolver at the riders, she advanced toward them. But nothing happened! Many times she had seen Sulky aim a weapon and it would fire. But the revolver shook lifelessly in her grasp. Maybe she could bluff them even though she had been unable to conceal her fear from the owl.

They were hard men. She saw the flint in their eyes and heard the steel in their silence. Their horses were fagged, their eyes dilated and bloodshot from hard riding, and the only noise was of the mounts blowing and snorting, then pawing at the smell of water by the juniper. The men paid no more attention to her than if she were a bird, Dawn thought. She shook the pistol toward the riders, hoping it would go off and save her.

One mocked her with a hollow laugh and she aimed her weapon at the lanky shank of a man with rotten teeth clamping a cigarette and with stringy black hair sprouting from beneath a greasy hat. She shook the gun at them to make it go off, but the gun was as lifeless as the juniper behind her tormentors.

"Sulky will get you," she called, her hand tiring from holding the gun and the child fluttering wildly with the fear she could not shake. Both hands clasped the butt until a thumb wriggled free and rested on the pistol hammer. She squeezed the handle hard, but only the hammer gave and it snapped back into place with a click. Was this the secret of the revolver? Dawn shook it again, but it didn't fire.

The lanky man with the rotten teeth laughed again as he exhaled a serpentine ribbon of smoke at her. Dawn felt evil all around her and her ears pricked at the sound of dry grass rustling behind her. She twisted her neck quickly toward the wickiup just in time to see a massive hand come over her shoulder and grab her hands.

"Sulky," she screamed and the gun in her hand snapped, the hammer falling on an empty cylinder. The grip tightened around her wrists as taut as wet rawhide drying in a hot sun. The gun tumbled from her hand to the ground. Her ears rang with the laughter of the men about her and her face burned with the humiliation she feared was just beginning.

The lanky man with the rotten teeth came forward, tossing his cigarette at her feet, while the three still on horses dismounted. The man squeezing her hands into numbness came around her. He was a towering man, bearded and grim, with the strength of a grizzly. Beside him strode a lesser man, a patch over one eye and a gleaming knife in his hand.

When the big man released his grasp, Dawn flexed her numb fingers, uncertain they would move until she watched them wiggle. She was trembling and all the men except one — he held the reins to the horses and had an odd shape to his head — laughed at her. Dawn could feel the tears welling in her eyes and blurring the hideous face of the one-eyed man who held his knife up to her nose, then with its point traced a path from the tip of her nose, over her lips, under her chin and down her neck to the top of her dress. She felt a bead of blood trail down her neck and then felt his rough hand pull the neck of her dress from her body. He slipped the knife inside her dress and pulled against the buckskin which fell away on either side of the sharp blade. He squatted as the knife cut away the front of her dress. When he was done, he stood and pushed the dress to her shoulders. He licked his lips and the others — except the one holding the horses — laughed as they unhooked their belts and the buttons on their pants.

The big man shoved her to the ground, pulling the bearclaw necklace from her as she fell.

Stunned by the fall, Dawn tried to clear her mind of the confusion. Then she smelled the breath of the man with the rotten teeth close upon her and she knew the final humiliation had begun.

The owl had been right.

CHAPTER 2

Their bellies full of sweet mountain grass, the horses advanced over the diminishing foothills at a canter. Astride the black stallion Ember, Sulky rode as easily as if he were floating upon the animal's sleek back. And Ember, too, seemed almost to glide across the grassy slopes, his even strides steady, his wind strong, his sinewy muscles rippling through his shiny black hide like the breeze through the grass. Man and animal were almost one, Ember reacting instantly to the touch of Sulky's heel, the nudge of his knee or the cluck of his tongue. Strapped around Sulky's head was the antlered headdress he used to stalk deer and the white hide of a fresh kill was draped, fleshy side up, over Ember's satiny rump. Both man and animal seemed to revel in the success of the hunt, but behind them trotted the mare, the skinned carcass of a deer tied across her back. After the kill,

18

women always had work to do, but the mare, which Dawn had named Bonita, was as diligent with her chores as Dawn. But tanning this white hide for a robe would not bother Dawn because it would hold her child, Sulky's son, and keep him warm.

The heat of the bright western sun seeped through his checkered shirt, the warmth soothing the dull ache of the scar running from his right shoulder to his left hip. Though it had been many years since he had killed the grizzly, his back still remembered the bear's sharp claws and the trail they left through his flesh. Sometimes when he fired his carbine, its recoil sent an avalanche of pain coursing down the scar and at other times when his right arm carried a heavy load, a pain as hot as molten lead dripped along the scar.

The years had been hard on him, Sulky thought, but he was still alive and that was more than many Apache warriors could claim. The White Eyes had been too powerful to defeat. He had seen that and he had survived, but as an outcast from the Chiricahua. Despite that, he possessed a young and beautiful wife. Just half his fifty odd years, Dawn had soothed the aches of his many battle scars and had given him a peace he had never known. And soon, she would give him a son.

Occasionally, Sulky glanced back at Bonita, faithfully trailing him, carrying the albino's carcass as proudly as Ember wore the dead buck's hide. Behind him, Sulky saw the great clouds beginning to gather, then billowing above the mountains and reaching toward the sun. Finally, the clouds blotted out the sun and Sulky felt a chill run down his back, not along his scar, but down his spine. Maybe it was the sudden coolness of the cloud-spawned shade or maybe the first rumble of thunder that frightened him. Sulky was uncertain, so he touched the antlered headdress as if it might bring good luck. Glancing over his shoulder, he saw lightning flash among the mountaintops. The Thunder People had loosed their arrows and stormed among the mountains. Though the storm was far off, Sulky took up the cry of the nighthawk.

"Pee-ik, pee-ik," he called and Ember widened his stride, the changing pace causing the carbine hanging from a strap over Sulky's shoulder to hit the scar. "Pee-ik, pee-ik," Sulky cried again, imitating the nighthawk, a speckled bird that circled the skies on cloudy days and darted so swiftly that it could even outrace lightning.

As he repeated the nighthawk's cry, hoping the Thunder People, though still far away, would think him a bird and not come his way, Sulky thought of Dawn, uncertain if she would be frightened by the Thunder People. She was Mexican and, though she had lived most of her life as an Apache, she held onto some of her beliefs from before she was stolen. Sometimes she doubted the beliefs of the Apache. Though she was often silent in her doubts, Sulky could read them in her eyes. And it worried him.

"Pee-ik, pee-ik," he called again. Then it happened.

A tremor came so slight at the corner of his eye that he tried to ignore it.

Even so, cold chills seemed to pulse with the blood through his body.

The tremor returned, now stronger and undeniable.

He caught his breath and held it for a moment, forgetting the Thunder People, forgetting that he was a nighthawk.

Another spasm, as light as a sparrow's breath, started at the corner of his right eye, then moved in successive trembles down his cheek until his face felt like the surface of a windswept water hole.

Sulky released his hot breath. It was a terrible sign, the tremor. It meant someone close to him would die. There was no one close to him now, except Dawn.

Dawn!

He wished for ashes that he might rub in his eye for sometimes that would forestall death. But here between the mountains and his home, no one would camp, no one would build a fire. He took up the chant that should accompany the application of ashes.

"Don't let this thing come to pass," he sang. "Don't let this thing come to pass."

The tremor continued.

"Don't let this thing come to pass," he cried.

His face numbed with the tremor.

"Don't let this thing come to pass," he screamed and the tremor was gone, but not his fear. It stabbed at him like a scalding dagger and he urged Ember ahead, faster, until the carbine bounced painfully against his back and Bonita, burdened by the carcass, fell behind.

Sulky rode low on Ember's neck, giving him rein and holding onto his silky mane, the antlered headdress sliding roughly on his head and galling his scalp. Just as the dawn came each day, he had grown accustomed to the constant presence of his own Dawn. What could the danger be?

Ember's ears twitched forward and Sulky

realized Ember had heard something. He shot upright on the horse's back and surveyed the countryside as he topped a hummock. There, a quarter mile to the north, he saw them.

Six riders.

They seemed in as big a hurry as he did, but like him they pulled up on their mounts and stared back. Ember fidgeted, pawing at the ground as Bonita caught up. They blew and snorted at one another and Sulky knew the animals understood. The six riders were bad men. Sulky touched the lucky antlers he wore on his head.

"Don't let this thing come to pass," he whispered, "don't let this thing come to pass." The horses calmed at his words, but Sulky could still feel the fear deep within himself, reaching all the way to the marrow in his bones.

The six riders halted on a hill, silhouetted against the sky like malevolent shadows. Sulky knew these men as he had known dozens previously — as enemies — but something made these more sinister. Perhaps it was the Thunder People behind him or the twitching muscle at his eye or, worse, what he would find when he reached Dawn. He pondered but an instant, for he must find Dawn. As he nudged Ember's flank

23

with his heels, he saw two riders jerking their rifles from scabbards. Bending low over Ember's neck, he saw the rifles exhale twin puffs of smoke and an instant later he heard the cough of the guns. But their aim was awry for he did not hear the whine of their bullets in the air or the thud when they found earth. It was good that they had shot at him, Sulky thought, for it meant they considered him a threat. If something were wrong with Dawn, they would have reason to be scared. They would remember the rider with antlers.

Ember lunged forward and Sulky slapped his neck, exhorting the animal to give his all. Bonita must surely be following, but Sulky no longer glanced behind to see. His eyes stared grimly from hillock to hillock until he spotted the hills surrounding his home. He slapped Ember harder now and kicked with his heel at the horse's flank.

"Please don't let this thing come to pass," he said a final time as he topped the little hill that hid his home.

Then he saw her. His stomach twisted in a knot unlike any other since he had had to kill his own brother. She was naked, her arms so contorted, her legs so widely spread, that she could only be dead. And dying with her, Sulky's son. His hand tightened around

24

Ember's mane until the stallion finally nickered at the pain and Sulky realized he was hurting his horse. He loosened his fingers, now pale from the exertion, and looked northward, the direction the men had gone. He would find them and they would die and he would mutilate them as they had his wife. And his son.

Bonita came racing up behind him, slowing a moment, then bolting over the hill toward the dead juniper and the water beneath its roots, but pulling up short when she caught the smell of blood. The mare stopped, tossing her head toward Dawn's body. Sulky nudged Ember forward. Now there was no hurry.

Instead of riding to Dawn, Sulky circled the chosa, staying inside the perimeter of the protecting hills. He found four sets of tracks coming in from the south. Across the way, he found two more sets of tracks, these coming from the west. The men had been of murderous intent from the beginning. Dawn had not had a chance. He continued circling Dawn's body in an ever tightening spiral. All the while, Bonita watched him, fidgeting under the weight of the deer carcass, and pawing but never moving in the direction of the water.

Nearing Dawn, Sulky dismounted and

pulled the white deer skin from Ember's back. His stomach was knotted tighter than before. He jerked the antlered headdress off his head, throwing it toward the gnarled juniper. Sulky screamed as if he were an old woman and jerked his knife from his scabbard. Reaching for his neck, he grabbed a handful of his shiny black hair, sliced it off and dropped it beside Dawn. Then kneeling beside her, he screamed again and patted her face.

Already she was cold and the day was still warm. She had been asleep and so pretty when he had left her this morning. Now she leaked between the legs from other men. The slash from a jagged knife snaked across her belly where the baby bulged slightly. From the ragged width of the shallow cut, Sulky could tell, the knife had a bent or broken blade. And between her breasts, he picked up the remains of a cigarette. He held it to his nose, taking in the tobacco smell and another vaguely familiar odor. It was the smell of rotting teeth. He remembered it well as a child held in the arms of Apache women whose teeth were dark and pitted. Standing up, Sulky noticed three more cigarette butts around Dawn. Picking them up to his nose, he sniffed at them all. The same man had smoked them as he waited his turn with Dawn.

Sulky slipped the cigarette butts in his shirt pocket. He vowed to kill the man who had slashed his wife's belly and his son. He vowed to kill the man who had smoked the cigarettes and left one between her breasts. If it were the same man, he would die two deaths.

Sulky spread out the white deer hide upon the ground and lifted Dawn upon it. She was so light and defenseless, but she must have tried. Under where she had lain, Sulky found his cap and ball pistol. Geronimo had given it to him many years ago for bravery before Sulky had turned against the Chiricahua. Even then it had not worked — otherwise Geronimo would have kept it — but no other warrior had ever been given a pistol by the great chief. He kept it in his pouch with his amulets so Dawn must have run to his wickiup to find it and protect herself. She would never have entered his wickiup unless she were desperate. He straightened her arms and legs in the hide and sprinkled her with his hair from the ground. Dissatisfied with that, he pulled his knife and cut another wad of hair, dropping it all upon her, then wrapping her in the robe.

He retreated to the chosa and slipped the

27

carbine from his shoulder and leaned it in the corner. He found a coal shuttle she used for cooking fires and went beside the chosa where the ground was not hard packed and dug a shallow grave. The work was hard and his right arm ached from the exertion. Would not that grizzly bear stop hurting him after all these years? Then it struck him. Dawn's bearclaw necklace — her proudest possession for how many wives had a husband who had killed a grizzly with his bare hands? — was missing from her neck. That bear, long dead, would claim one more man among its kills, Sulky vowed.

Finally the grave was dug, but not before Sulky's arm throbbed with spurts of pain. If he buried Dawn now, he could take up the trail of her murderers, Sulky thought. But he felt a stillness in the air and a hush among the wind and the animals. They, like him, feared the Thunder People. The great clouds were moving toward him and Sulky heard the thunder. He would wait here the night even if rains might make the trail of Dawn's murderers harder to find.

There was much to do before the storm hit. He rushed to Ember and Bonita, both grazing by the dead juniper and the water rocks, hobbled them both and cut the carcass free from the mare's back. He

28

shoved the carcass to the ground and examined the sores on her back where it had galled her. Then he found his antlered headdress and ran to his wickiup, gathering his pouch, his bow and his arrows and searching for his cartridge belt. But the murderers must have taken it, leaving him only with the bullets in his carbine and in his revolver. He emerged and retrieved his cap and ball pistol from the ground. Moving swiftly to the chosa, he piled everything in the corner by his carbine and near the pallet where he had slept with Dawn. He pulled two handsful of jerked venison from one of Dawn's baskets and shoved it in his pouch.

He was anxious to begin his hunt, but he would not challenge the Thunder People, not today. It was not that he feared death, just dying before he killed his wife's murderers.

Sulky slipped outside, hoping the Thunder People would not notice, but as he reached Dawn's corpse, a flash of lightning and the crash of thunder showed he had been seen. He picked up Dawn's light form and carried her gently to the grave. Lowering her into the ground, he thought of his son who would never be and he seemed to go numb, holding Dawn for a long time just above the grave's bottom and finally, when his right arm felt as if it might fall off into the grave with her, letting go. Dawn slipped away.

He picked up the shuttle, but his arm still throbbed. Then he remembered a burial he had seen at Fort Bowie when a soldier on firewood detail had been killed. The soldiers had lined up over his grave and fired their guns into the air.

It seemed the right thing to do, even though he was running short on ammunition. His right hand quivering from the pain, he pulled his pistol from its holster and held it to the sky, careful not to point it in the direction of the Thunder People. He squeezed off five unevenly spaced shots for Dawn. And, for his son.

CHAPTER 3

Whit reined up on his chestnut, his free hand falling instinctively to his Colt .45 Peacemaker.

Silas pulled up his mount beside Whit. "What's the . . ." he started and immediately realized he should've held his tongue.

Whit, his head tilting toward the north, held up his hand for silence and stared hard at Silas. Whit's burning glare scalded Silas until he shifted nervously in his saddle, the resulting squeak of leather bringing a flare of aggravation to Whit's gray eyes.

Feeling Whit's scorching gaze but hearing only thunder, Silas tugged the brim of his Stetson over his eyes and waited. Then he heard the gunshots, two of them, and raised his head. Damn Whit! The contrary old fart never missed a thing, Silas begrudged him that, but traveling with him was as touchy as a toothache and not nearly as satisfying.

Silas waited, listening to the whisper of

his breath and the thump of his heart and figuring both were too loud for Whit's liking. In five hard days on the trail, Silas had learned Whit would speak — eventually — so he just waited, frozen in the saddle so the leather wouldn't squeak. The seconds seemed to inch by. Silas's nose crawled with a terrible itch that needed scratching and his throat twitched from a film of trail dust that needed coughing up. But to make noise now might be as deadly as catching up with the Bastrop gang because Whit had that no-nonsense look in his gray eyes. Maybe that was why Whit had survived as a marshal more than fifteen years in Arizona and now New Mexico Territory.

To the west thunder rolled down the mountains, rumbling like a freight wagon out of control. Under the cover of the thunder, Silas shifted in his saddle and took a swipe at the infernal itch on his nose, running his forearm across his nostrils, raising a puff of dust from his sleeve. It thundered again and Silas spit the scratchiness from his throat, but it came back when he swallowed. He craved the water in his canteen, but he'd not steal a drop unless Whit sipped some of his own. Silas must conserve his water because Whit didn't take kindly to delays when he took scent of his prey and going out of the way for water would slow him. Silas didn't relish riding into that storm, but darned if rain wouldn't taste sweet upon his dry tongue.

Finally, Whit reached into his vest pocket and pulled out a plug of chewing tobacco. No wonder Whit was seldom thirsty, Silas thought, because he was always sucking on that wad of cud. There was a trail of Whit's tobacco juice all the way back to the Texas border where they had picked up the tracks of the train robbers. It wasn't until they reached Mesilla they learned they were trailing the Bastrop gang.

Whit whittled free a couple of tobacco slivers and folded his knife, shoving it and the plug back in his vest pocket. When he took new tobacco, Whit usually was on the verge of speaking. But first, he cogitated deeply, his brow furrowing, eyes narrowing, lips tightening as if deciding how few words he could use to communicate. Whit was as stingy with words as he was with his canteen water.

Silas waited, knowing Whit would find fault with him for something. When the words came, Silas flinched.

"How many shots?"

Turning to stare back at Whit, Silas shrugged, knowing the instant he did that it was a mistake. "Two's all I heard."

With disgust, Whit spat a stream of tobacco juice between their horses. "Five shots! When I stop, you don't be asking questions."

Silas nodded, doubting he could ever suit Whit, not the way Zack always had. "You figure it's the Bastrop gang?"

Whit stroked his chin between his thumb and forefinger. "Reckon not. They know they ain't given us the slip and there's too little cover to draw us into an ambush."

"They'll head back into the mountains . . ." Silas started, his voice tightening at the remembrance of Zack, buried back on the trail, ". . . and bushwhack us there like they did before?"

Whit just stared. Silas detected no emotion in the marshal's eyes. Zack had ridden a decade with Whit, though Silas couldn't understand why. Zack was easygoing, talkative, even friendly, everything that Whit was not. Ten years they had ridden together, saved each other's hides a dozen times, brought in some of the most feared men in Arizona and New Mexico Territories, had eaten from the same plate, had even shared the same woman on occasion. And now, Whit seemed not even to remember his partner.

Silas couldn't think of the ambush without having to acknowledge Zack's existence. "God rest his soul," Silas sighed. "And his widow."

"She cared for his monthly pay, not him," Whit said, nudging his chestnut forward.

Advancing with him, Silas waited for instructions. After a hundred yards of silence, Whit spoke. "About half a mile to where I figure the shots were fired. Keep about seventy-five feet between us. Stay ready with your carbine."

Silas nodded and tugged the reins of his bay away. He watched Whit pull his Winchester from its saddle boot and he did likewise, cradling the gun barrel in the crook of his left arm and slipping his finger across the trigger. He took in the gentle swell of the hills ahead and enjoyed the cool breeze the giant thunderstorm was pushing down the mountains and over the foothills, carrying with it the gentle aroma of rain. His bay caught the smell of water and took up a livelier pace. Silas kept Whit in the corner of his eye and held back his horse so that he topped each rise the same time as the marshal.

At the top of the fourth hillock, Silas pulled up in surprise. Below in a natural bowl surrounded by shallow hills stood a primitive house, a chosa. Damn fool place for a white man to build a home, Silas thought as he sat waiting for Whit to ride down the hillside. Two hobbled horses standing beside a dead juniper tree stared back. Nearby lay a carcass, possibly a deer. And near the chosa, Silas took in a brush wickiup like the Apaches built. Then he saw a man, by his dress an Apache, on his knees and motionless beside a pit at the chosa's side. As Silas watched, he realized Whit was halfway down the hill, his carbine back in its scabbard. Silas held his carbine at the ready though. Indians still made him nervous even if their threat had ended a half dozen years ago. Silas clucked his tongue and kicked his bay into a trot, the sound of his hooves catching the Indian's attention. Silas watched the Indian lift his head, then stand. Silas glanced at Whit, but the marshal stared steadfastly at the Indian. Silas reined in his mount a bit so he would not approach the Indian before Whit.

The marshal sat easy in the saddle, his hands resting on the saddlehorn. As Whit reached the Indian, he gave all indications of spitting, then seemed to hold back on the stream of tobacco juice long enough that Silas half wished he'd choke on it. Then Silas saw the reason for Whit's sudden surge of manners. It was not a pit, but a grave the man now stood beside. At his feet lay a woman, wrapped in a white skin. Death had hardened the soft curves of the woman's face and her lips were a pasty purple, reminding Silas of Zack's lips when he and Whit had finally been able to bury him day before yesterday. Like Zack, the woman had not died of old age, but of violence, most likely the latest victim on the death list being written by the Bastrop gang.

Silas looked from the woman to the man. He did not carry grief in his black eyes, but revenge. He stood a couple of inches under six feet, but he stood straight, his square chin jutting forward in challenge, his high cheekbones accentuating the vindictive eyes, his hollow cheeks giving him a hungry look. His narrow downturned lips appeared carved in stone from many smileless years and his ragged black hair gave him an evil look. The Indian wore a red checked shirt, khaki pants covered by a breechcloth and leather leggings reaching to his knee. Silas studied the empty cartridge belt around the Indian's waist, wondering if the pistol on his right side was as empty and how good he was with the knife on his left side. Because the Indian faced him instead of Whit, Silas felt safer cradling the carbine.

"Who did this, Apache friend?"

Silas wondered how Whit knew the Indian was Apache. He stared at the marshal for a clue and was surprised by the intensity on Whit's face, almost as great as it had been when they had buried Zack.

"Six White Eyes," the Apache said, his voice low and sinister, his head turned to avoid Whit's stare.

Whit nodded and held open his vest to reveal his badge, tarnished from years without a polishing, but the Indian didn't look. "I'm tracking the bad men. Was it their shots I heard a short time ago? Five shots?"

The Apache shook his head. "White Eyes kill her while me in mountains hunting. I return, they riding away. I shoot gun over grave like soldiers at Fort Bowie."

"Fort Bowie," Whit said, mostly to himself as he stroked his whisker-stubbled jaw with his thumb and forefinger. Then Whit spat and dug into his vest pocket for his tobacco plug and knife to reload his chaw.

It hadn't been that long since Whit had given himself fresh tobacco, Silas thought. Something must be bothering him about the Indian. Silas studied Whit's hard stare and was surprised by Whit's next question.

"Apache friend, you ever see me before?"

The Indian bent down and picked up a

small coal scoop and began raking the freshly turned dirt back over the woman. "I see many White Eyes. Sleep better not remembering them."

"Lift the back of your shirt, Apache friend," Whit ordered softly.

Silas recognized the challenge in Whit's voice, but the Apache ignored it, as he covered the woman, a scoop of dirt at a time. Silas watched the Apache and saw him tense at the click of the hammer on Whit's single action Colt. Out of the corner of his eye, he could see Whit waving his revolver at the Indian.

"Lift the back of your shirt, Apache friend."

The Indian threw down the scoop, stared for a moment at the gun, then looked straight into Whit's face. Silas, figuring the Indian was planning to fight, reined his horse around so the barrel of his carbine was pointed at the Indian.

Slowly, the Indian nodded and turned around, jerking his shirt from beneath the cartridge belt and lifting it to his shoulder. Silas winced at the sight, a ragged purple and pink scar running from his right shoulder to his left waist.

"Okay, Apache friend," Whit said. "You ever scout for the Army?"

The sullen Indian tucked his shirt under the cartridge belt and picked up the scoop to continue his chore. "I scout, you know I scout, Bill Whitman."

Silas felt his jaw drop open. He shot a quick glance at Whit. Silas and most others knew the marshal only as Whit, short for Whitman, but here was an Apache in the middle of nowhere calling him by his seldom-used first name. As imperturbable as ever, Whit lolled in the saddle, for a moment neither acknowledging nor denying the Apache's claim, then reholstered his Colt.

"Was she your woman, Sulky?"

The Indian grunted and worked faster as the sound of thunder grew louder and the breeze kicked up the dust. "You trail bad White Eyes?" Sulky asked, without looking up from the grave. "Good scout, you need. Country rough. I know way."

Whit spat a stream of tobacco juice away from the grave, but he held his words.

Silas's thumb fidgeted with the hammer on his carbine and he felt an uneasiness spreading like a stain across his chest. He didn't rightly like the idea of an Apache traveling with him, even if it did improve the odds with the Bastrop gang.

Sulky, as Whit called the Indian, finished

40

mounding dirt over his wife's grave, and still the marshal had not answered him. The Apache stood over the grave, looking skyward, the scoop sliding from his fingers. He lifted his arms to the sky in some mysterious ritual, then let them fall to his side, uncomfortably close to his revolver, Silas thought.

The Apache then stared fiercely at the marshal. "Sulky, good scout," he said. "I get letter Red Beard give to Sulky." The Indian trotted between the two lawmen to the front of the chosa, Silas watching him disappear around the corner and expecting him to return with guns ablaze. Whit dismounted, spit out all his tobacco, unstrapped his canteen and took a healthy swig of water, swishing it around in his mouth, then shaking his head as he swallowed. Silas managed a raspy swallow at the burning dryness in his jealous throat, but felt safer having his carbine at the ready than trying to quench his thirst just yet. Silas flinched at a flash of lightning and the exploding thunder. He glanced to the west and saw the storm was passing north of them. When he looked back, Sulky stood at his feet and Silas felt a shiver as cold as ice plunge down his spine.

Sulky's cold glare, as his hand plunged into a wide leather pouch, did little to melt the uneasiness Silas felt. Extracting a yellowed piece of paper, dog-eared at the corners, Sulky handed it to Whit.

The marshal plugged his canteen and took the paper, studying it several seconds. Whit nodded, then stepped to Silas and offered him the letter. "Red Beard write truth about Sulky," the marshal said.

Not wanting to exchange his grip on his carbine for the letter, Silas waved the paper away. That was a mistake, Silas realized, when Whit's eyes narrowed and his hand shook the paper again. Silas reached for the letter, half expecting the Apache to strike with snake quickness. Sulky folded his arms across his chest as if he were proud Whit was forcing Silas to read the letter.

The carbine still cradled in the crook of his left arm, Silas held the letter, a hand on each side so it wouldn't flop in the breeze. The letter was written on U.S. Army paper and it was signed, to Silas's surprise, by Gen. George Crook. Silas studied the fading ink. "To whom it may concern, the Apache Sulky has served me four years as a scout. As a scout, he may have an equal, but none is better. Even so, he is treacherous and I do not entirely trust him." The letter closed with the general's signature.

Silas folded the letter and offered it to

Whit. The marshal grabbed Silas's hand and held it for an instant as he accepted the yellowing paper. When Whit spoke, Silas knew it was directed at him, not Sulky. "Red Beard," Whit said, "wrote truth about Sulky."

Sulky stood with his feet spread apart, his arms folded across his chest, his chin jutting defiantly forward. He nodded slowly at Whit's words. "Sulky, good scout. Red Beard like. Now, Sulky scout for you. Find bad men."

If the red fool could read Crook's paper, Silas thought, he'd know Whit'd never take him on as scout. Then Whit spoke and Silas's notion clabbered like bad milk in his brain.

"We can use a good scout," Whit said, "but he's gotta follow my orders, just like in the Army. We take bad men back alive. No revenge."

Sulky unfolded his arms and nodded.

Whit looked northward and shook his head at the storm. "Our horses need rest and water. We'll stay the night and leave before sunrise."

"Sulky follow orders, Bill Whitman. Like old days, huh?"

"Like the old days, Sulky. Now, where's the nearest water?"

43

The Indian pointed to the twisted juniper and the rocks at its roots. "Dead tree leak good water."

Whit took the reins of his chestnut and stepped that way. Silas stared at Sulky a moment more, then turned his horse toward the juniper, waiting until he passed Whit to dismount.

When Whit reached him, Silas, his carbine still in hand, fell in step with the marshal, walking his horse toward water. "Didn't you read the letter?" Silas whispered.

"Nothing I didn't know."

"And you're taking him on? I don't trust him."

"You've reason not to." Whit nodded and spit out a noise that was the bastard offspring between a cough and a laugh. "At Fort Bowie, he once brought in the heads of his brother and an uncle and dumped them out of a tow sack onto the parade ground." Silas felt his throat tighten, but not from thirst.

"That scar on his back," Whit continued, "came from an encounter with a grizzly, an encounter Sulky won with his bare hands and his knife."

"But why're you taking him on?" Silas asked, ashamed of the fear he detected in his own voice.

Whit turned quiet until they reached the juniper and the horses took drink from the little pool of cloudy water there.

"Money, Silas, reward money."

"Huh?"

"All but one in the Bastrop gang has a price on his head. Ben Bastrop alone is worth five hundred. The rest of them, except for the kid that ain't right in the head, they're worth good money too. I don't stand a chance of getting those rewards if Sulky goes after them. He'll find them and he'll kill them for what they did to his woman. What he leaves of their bodies won't be enough for me to claim a reward and the rail company won't pay up just on my word. If Sulky rides with us, maybe I can take a couple of them alive and earn the rewards."

Silas shrugged. "If Sulky don't kill *us* first."

CHAPTER 4

At first Dummy didn't understand Ben Bastrop was yelling at him. Over the last five days of hard riding, exhaustion had seeped into every fiber of his muscles and he ached so much it pained him even to sleep. And his mind no longer worked as well as it could.

Of course, the others didn't think he had much of a mind. But he knew right from wrong. Robbing trains was wrong, but holding the horses was okay. Dummy hadn't stopped the train, hadn't shot open the express car door, hadn't killed the railway clerk. He'd just held the horses and then ridden away with the Bastrop gang. They weren't good men, but they let him ride with them and no good man had ever done that. They weren't good men, but they'd given him a pistol which no good man had ever trusted him with. Many times in the dark when strange noises frightened him,

46

Dummy would rub the pistol tucked in his pants and feel safer, even if it was missing the trigger and hammer and even if he didn't have any bullets for it.

"Dummy," Ben Bastrop yelled again.

Hearing his name, Dummy sat up on his blanket, shivering in his wet clothes, wishing he'd had a slicker like the others when the thunderstorm had struck. He snapped the middle finger on his left hand like he always did when he was nervous. Turning around on his blanket, Dummy watched Bastrop fling his arms out and speak, his words made visible by the cigarette smoke he exhaled as he issued orders.

"Dummy," Bastrop called, "you need to use your ears. I've got a chore for you."

His finger snapping faster, Dummy stared beyond Bastrop at the scattered junipers and piñon pines on the mountains. He was glad to be back in the mountains where there were more hiding places than on the prairie. Dummy had wanted desperately to hide this afternoon after he had seen that deer riding a horse before the thunderstorm. The others had said it was a single Indian wearing deer antlers and a hide draped over his head, but Dummy couldn't understand if they were teasing him or telling the truth. They needled him a lot and sometimes it

47

was hard to tell.

"Dummy, go find us some firewood," Bastrop commanded. "Maybe we can fire up enough coffee to break the chill from the rain. You hear me, boy?"

Nodding, Dummy arose slowly, his aches climbing from the blanket with him, his finger snapping weakly. As he stood, he saw Bastrop grin, his cigarette clamped between brown, putrid teeth, the smoke curling like a vaporous serpent toward the now cloudless sky. Bastrop always smoked and issued orders and picked on him, Dummy thought.

Bastrop ran his fingers through his stringy black hair, then scratched his scraggly beard which sprouted in coils over his face. His beady eyes, deepset in their sockets and half hidden amid the hair, studied Dummy. "Well, boy, you gonna get moving or am I gonna have to whup you?" Bastrop sneered as if he'd enjoy that.

Dummy's finger snapped quicker, harder against his palm, and he wanted to say something, but what? He was pondering hard on an answer when Pete stepped to his side and faced Bastrop.

Tall and lean, his whiskerless face pockmarked by smallpox, Pete lifted his hand, patting Dummy's shoulder. In a moment Dummy realized his nervous finger was still.

Dummy liked Pete because Pete would talk to him and answer his questions without angering and Pete would sometimes take his Bible and read to him stories about King David and Jesus.

"Hold on, Dummy," Pete said, his voice as gentle as his touch. "Now, Ben, everybody except Dummy knows he's not gonna find any dry wood now, not after the showers this afternoon. He'd look all night for dry wood and you'd laugh yourself to sleep over that."

Ben jerked his spit-stained cigarette from his mouth, his eyes flaring with rage.

Sometimes Dummy feared Ben might hurt Pete, but the most Bastrop ever seemed to muster was threats.

"Pete, who runs this outfit?" Bastrop flicked his cigarette at Dummy, then stuck his thumbs in his gunbelt. "Who's boss?"

"Being boss and being fair aren't the same, Ben," Pete answered, his voice as calm as a water hole on a windless day. "Dummy don't understand these things. And the rest of us know you wouldn't build a fire with damp wood. The smoke'd draw Whit Whitman here as quick as you could boil your coffee."

Ben grunted and turned to the others. "Any of you want warm coffee?"

Leander cinched the hobble on his gray's foreleg and twisted his head toward Ben. "Sure, Ben, I want some hot coffee. And, how about a beefsteak and some taters to go with it. Maybe some bread dripping with fresh-churned butter. And when that's done, some apple pie." He grinned. "If you can't get all the other, then I'll do without the coffee." Leander stood straight, patting the gray on the neck.

Ben scowled, then nodded at Claude. "How 'bout you?"

"Coffee'd be good, but I don't wanna let Whitman know our whereabouts. I'm don't want to shoot with him again. I make a bigger target than the rest of you."

Dummy nodded. Claude was a mountain of a man, all muscle and gristle, easy on his friends but hard on horses. A man his size wore out horses quicker than a lesser man so he always traveled with an extra mount to switch to on long rides. Claude wore a red flannel shirt over a blue-checked one as if one shirt were not big enough for his girth. Dummy wished he were Claude's size because the big man spoke little, except when spoken to, and yet no one made fun of his silence like they did his own.

Ben pulled his hat down over his forehead until his beady eyes were harder to see than those of a snake in a rocky crevice. He snarled toward Prentice who was already chewing on a sliver of dried beef. "You with me, Prent?"

Prentice, sitting on the ground on his saddle and cleaning his nails with the point of his Bowie knife, glanced up from his fingers at Ben, then Pete. "No fires, Ben, not as long as you keep the money in your saddlebags. Once we divide the money and split up, you can fire the whole countryside for all I care." With the tip of the knife, he scratched his left brow where his leather eyepatch had rubbed a callus. Then he held the knife up to the sky, studying the blade where the bullet had hit it. After the robbery, a lucky shot had struck him at the hip. But instead of piercing flesh, the bullet had hit his scabbard, boogering the knife near the point. "No fires, Ben."

"Ben, no one wants a fire," Pete said.

Dummy detected a challenge in Pete's voice, but didn't understand it since Pete and Ben were brothers of some kind. Stepbrothers, he recalled without understanding what that meant. The two sure didn't look like brothers of any kind, Pete being on the heavier side with thick blond hair. He might have been handsome except for the smallpox scars on his face. But Dummy most liked

51

Pete's soft eyes and his calm reasoning.

"Like Prent said," Pete continued, "no fires until we split the money."

"I've said it before, Pete," Ben said, noting Pete's challenge with reciprocated contempt, "we're safer as long as we stay together. No place around here worth spending the money."

Dummy nodded, thinking of the ten dollars Ben had promised him for holding the horses. It'd been days since Dummy had seen a store. He knew how he would spend his money. Licorice! He'd buy every stick of licorice in the candy jar if he could just find a store. And if Ben would ever give him his money.

Ben mumbled. "Coffee'd sure be good for a change." Then he shrugged at the lack of support and walked away.

As Ben strode away from the circle of bedrolls on the ground, Dummy sat back down on his damp blankets, shivering, and Pete wandered away.

Dummy had intended to thank Pete for aiding him, but Pete now seemed busy unfolding his bedroll and stretching it out beside his saddle, then picking up a wad of clothing from the middle where he kept his Bible. As Pete pulled a shirt and britches from the clothes bundle, the Bible fell free and Dummy hoped Pete was going to read him a story. But Pete left the Bible on the blanket and tossed Dummy some clothes. Dummy dodged, then felt silly, realizing Pete was only trying to help him. Dummy caught the pants, but the shirt dropped at his feet.

"Change into those, Dummy," Pete said, his voice soothing, "and I'll hang your wet ones on a juniper to dry."

Dummy struggled to answer, his words coming out in mumbles the first time, then coherently, but softly, so the others might not hear and make fun of him. "Thanks, Pete."

Pete nodded. "Then I'll read you a story."

Dummy clapped his hands, then began to undress, pulling his broken revolver from his pants and dropping it on his blanket, taking off his shoes and pants, then his shirt until he stood, lacking underwear, with only a pair of socks on. He feared the others would laugh at him. They had laughed this afternoon at the woman when she was naked before them. Dummy never remembered seeing a naked woman, except maybe his little sister when she was just a girl. He had shared the woman's shame at her nakedness and he had puzzled over how the men had treated her. But even so, he had found himself fascinated by the gentle sweep of her flesh and by the lush curves of her hips and breasts and all the time he had just wanted to stare at her body, without the others lunging wildly atop her.

Ben Bastrop had lain twice upon her and Dummy hated him doubly for it. Dummy knew right from wrong and what they had done to her was wrong, even if he didn't understand what it was.

Dummy scrambled into Pete's spare change of clothes, glad he was dressed again and wondering if the woman had ever awakened. She had slept so soundly that she did not move, even when Ben Bastrop left a burning cigarette between her breasts or when Prent had taken his knife and scratched her flesh. He hoped she was better now and wished he could forget what they had done to her, but every time Claude moved, the woman's bearclaw necklace clicked against itself around his neck and Dummy remembered.

As Pete took Dummy's clothes and spread them over the branches of a nearby juniper, Dummy slid down on his blanket, his muscles trembling with exhaustion. Ben Bastrop strolled by, muttering something inconsequential. Dummy took to snapping his finger, expecting Bastrop to insult him, but he passed on by, Dummy's eyes following his every step until his finger relaxed. When he looked around toward the south from where they had ridden, he realized Pete was beside him, offering him a piece of jerky and a dried apple slice with one hand and holding his Bible with the other. Dummy grabbed the food, sticking the jerky in his mouth, sucking on its leathery sweetness, saving the dried apple and wishing it and the dried meat were licorice.

The candle was burning low on another day and about him Dummy could hear quail calling. As Pete sat down beside him, Dummy scanned the silhouette of the low mountain to the west and then he froze in fear. His finger began snapping against his palm and he could feel his shoulder trembling. Outlined against the pastel sky, he saw a deer, one with broad antlers. Was it the deer he had seen riding horseback earlier? He pointed with trembling fingers. "Peeete," his throat quivered.

Dummy felt Pete's hand rest on, then pat his shoulder. "Good eyes, Dummy," Pete said. "It's a deer."

Nodding, Dummy knew that. But was it the deer which had terrorized him earlier this afternoon?

"It's not the one you saw on a horse," Pete

55

said, his voice soothing.

Dummy sighed and the trembling slipped away, but still he watched the buck for several seconds until the animal shook his antlers and started down the opposite side of the mountain.

"Now, Dummy, would you like a story?"

Clapping his hands softly so the deer might not realize he was near, Dummy nodded. He liked to hear Pete's stories about Moses and Noah and Jesus. They reminded him of when his ma had read to him as a child, but she had had other children, children that were smarter. His ma had cared for him and even loved him, but Dummy knew that he shamed her by his dumbness. She was pretty, prettier than all his sisters even, his mother was, and she had tolerated his dumbness, though he could often sense in her voice the frustration he caused her. Dummy might never have run away from home except for his little sister. She was littler by three years and he always had figured she'd never get as smart as himself. But that had changed and for some reason she had seemed to grow much smarter while he stayed the same. He had run away in disgrace and finally taken up with these men. He would've left them, except for Pete.

"Let me read you a story, Dummy, before the light is gone and we must sleep," Pete said, thumbing through his Bible worn from reading and from portage in a bedroll. "Do you know of Solomon? He was a wise man, some say the wisest man that God ever created."

Dummy touched his finger to his lips and Pete knew to read. Pete turned a couple more pages in his Bible and took to reading about God appearing to Solomon in a dream and asking him what gift he wanted. And King Solomon had asked for wisdom. Dummy wished God would come to him tonight in a dream so he could ask for smarts and could return proudly home to his mother. He wanted that more than even a jar of licorice.

" 'Then came there unto the King two women, that were harlots,' " Pete said and the other men laughed, though Dummy did not understand why, " 'and stood before him.' "

Pete read on, but Dummy felt confused by the laughter of the others. It was not a funny story, two women each with child until one had died. Now both women stood before the wise Solomon claiming the surviving baby. It was confusing.

" 'Then said the king,' " Pete continued,

his voice rising like a stump preacher, " 'The one saith, This is my son that liveth, and thy son is the dead; and the other saith, Nay; but thy son is the dead, and my son is the living.

" 'And the king said, Bring me a sword,' " Pete said, stopping to explain a sword was a big knife. Dummy looked at Prentice, still carving on his nails with his bowie knife and shuddered. " 'And they brought a sword before the king.

" 'And the king said, Divide the living child in two, and give half to the one and half to the other.

" 'Then spake the woman whose the living child was unto the king, for her bowels yearned upon her son, and she said, O my lord, give her the living child, and in no wise slay it. But the other said, Let it be neither mine nor thine, but divide it.

" 'Then the king answered and said, Give her the living child, and in no wise slay it. She is the mother thereof. And all Israel heard of the judgment and they feared the king for they saw that the wisdom of God was in him.' " Pete paused for a moment, then slowly closed the Bible.

Dummy liked the story and envied Solomon his wisdom, but he disliked the others laughing yet. He was confused if they laughed at him or at Pete, but surely they must not laugh at Solomon because he was too smart, like Dummy wanted to he.

"Dummy," called Ben Bastrop.

"Don't start in on him, Ben," Pete replied as he stood in the gathering darkness and eased over to his pallet.

But Bastrop never seemed to hear because he kept talking and Dummy realized he was snapping his finger again.

"Dummy, you know what a harlot is?"

That word? Pete had read it in the story but Dummy had never heard it before.

"A harlot?" Bastrop repeated.

From the shadows of day's end Dummy could hear the other men laughing, all except Pete.

"Do you, Dummy?"

Dummy's tongue seemed paralyzed with fear and he struggled for the answer, his reply coming first as a gurgle, then a cough. He shook his head.

"A harlot's a woman like we all had this afternoon, all of us excepting you."

Dummy could see the woman and remember the fear in her eyes and, most troubling of all, her appealing nakedness. He felt a cold sweat upon his forehead and feared that Bastrop would laugh more.

"Shutup, Ben," Pete demanded.

"You ever had a woman, Dummy?" Ben laughed as he spoke.

Dummy felt proud that he had had a woman and that Bastrop would not trick him this time. He fought against his tongue to answer. "Yep," he stammered, "I . . . I . . . I had a ma and three sisters."

His ears burned from the sudden burst of laughter coming at him from all directions. All of them laughed, except Pete, their laughter coming not as a sprinkle but as a torrent until it seemed to echo off the mountains. And Dummy could not understand for there was nothing wrong with having a mother and three sisters. He sank down onto his blanket and felt the tears stinging his eyes. He tried to unravel the knotted threads in his mind, but he could make no sense of why they had laughed at him, at his ma, at his sisters. And long after Bastrop had returned from the first watch, Dummy squirmed upon his thin blanket upon the hard ground, trying to understand why the others always laughed at him.

CHAPTER 5

"Hellfire and brimstone," Whit muttered and Silas jerked awake.

Silas rubbed his eyes, then felt his throat. Sure enough, his neck was still attached between his head and shoulders. He'd survived his first night with Sulky.

"Hellfire and brimstone," Whit repeated and Silas realized trouble had struck. Whit didn't air his lungs much, being stingy even with cusswords, but when he did the worst he'd spout was hellfire and brimstone. But Silas held his tongue in check, knowing Whit'd address him when he wanted to talk.

Then Whit whistled, a loud shrill whistle that shattered the quiet of the morning just now softening around the edges with light.

Silas covered his ears with his hands as Whit whistled again. What was the fuss about? Silas wondered what Sulky was thinking of this. Twisting over his blanket, Silas stared toward the corner where Sulky had stacked his carbine, pistol, bow and arrows, pouch, deerhead skin with antlers and his bedding, but it was too dark to see much. Turning to Whit, Silas could barely see the marshal, reclining on his bedroll in front of the door.

Whit said, "Silas, you like to walk?"

The question didn't make sense, but few things did with Whit. "What, Whit?"

"Hellfire and brimstone, do you like to walk? Sulky's left."

Silas sat up on his blanket and twisted around to the corner where Sulky had slept. The gentle morning light had softened the shadows enough that Silas could see that Sulky and his belongings were gone. But still, it didn't fit. "Walk? What's wrong with riding?"

"Sulky's taken our horses!"

Then Silas understood. Whit hadn't been whistling out of contrariness, but to call his horse as he had seen him do after letting the hobbled horse graze through the night. The chestnut would always come at the sound of his whistle, but not today. Silas felt a sinking in his stomach, wondering if there wasn't better work than being a deputy marshal. In a way it was funny, Whit throwing his pallet by the door so Sulky would have to crawl over him to get out.

And yet the Apache had done it, carrying all his belongings with him. Silas smiled to himself, glad Whit could not see him in the dark shadows. "Thought that's why you slept by the door, Whit."

"Hellfire and brimstone!" Whit seemed to choke on the profane admission of his oversight. "Only Sulky could've gotten past me."

"Well, Whit, it appears he did," Silas answered, enjoying Whit's discomfort for a change, but figuring he'd pressed his luck enough or Whit just might plug him and bury him outside with the dead squaw.

Whit raised up and reached for his boots, shaking each out, then pulling them over his feet. For several minutes, he stared outside and Silas could only guess at his thoughts. Shortly, his hands went instinctively to his vest pocket and he pulled out his knife and began to whittle away on his tobacco plug. By good light, he was working on a cheek-bulging chaw. Silas called this first chaw breakfast, for Whit wasn't much of an eater and was usually mounted and ready to ride just about the time the hunger pains were gnawing at Silas's belly. But this morning, they'd have time to fry some saltpork, unless Whit figured he could chase down the Bastrop gang afoot.

After Whit sidled outside for his morning leak, Silas pushed himself up from his blanket, working the stiffness out of his arms, then slipping his boots over his sore feet and dancing a little jig until his feet felt right in his boots. He gathered his two blankets and rolled them up inside his tarp, tying it all up with a couple of leather thongs and tossing it out the door. As he leaned his carbine against the door, he noticed a couple of baskets on a bench against the wall by the corner fireplace. The room was so scarcely furnished — a bench against each wall, a stool, a couple of pots and a stack of thick robes for a bed — that Silas was surprised he hadn't seen the baskets yesterday. But then, he'd been worried about Sulky. Damn if he wasn't glad that Sulky had escaped, even if it meant he was afoot with Whit now. Silas returned inside to the bench and sat down by the baskets, picking one up and tilting it until the lid slid to the floor. The basket was filled with fine strips of jerked meat. Pulling a slice out, he held it up to his nose. No telling what an Apache was likely to eat. It didn't smell any ranker than other jerked meats he had eaten, so he stuck it in his mouth to let it soften. He knew the taste — venison. He knocked the lid off the second basket, but the foul aroma quickly convinced him he should explore it no more. Carrying the basket of jerky outside, he met Whit coming from around the corner.

"Jerky?" Silas offered, holding the basket out to Whit.

The marshal waved it away. "Hellfire and brimstone," he answered and Silas knew Whit was still fuming over letting Sulky get away.

Though his lip quivered with the threat of a grin, Silas nodded without emotion and dropped the basket beside his bedroll, then hauled his saddle and saddle bags outside. Uncovering the basket, he shoved a handful in his britches pocket, then stuffed his saddlebags with more and left the basket by Whit's gear in case he wanted any. While Whit paced around the cabin, walking out his anger, Silas sauntered over to the juniper and sat on the mound of rocks, dipping his cupped hand periodically into the pool of cool water and enjoying its sweetness.

For several minutes, Silas enjoyed the morning's cool stillness. A man could come to love this country, if he spent enough time studying its moods and learning from it, Silas thought, but his contemplation was interrupted by Whit calling for him. Silas scooped up another handful of water and stood up, thinking how this hard country was easier to like than Whit. "Yeah," Silas answered, starting the marshal's way.

"Move your gear out by the tree," called Whit, himself loaded with bridle, saddle, saddlebags, bedroll, canteen and carbine.

Taking the order in silence, Silas walked up to his belongings, noticing the basket had as much jerky in it as when he had left it for Whit. He retrieved another strip and jammed it in his mouth, then carried his gear away, unsure why Whit had decided his belongings should be moved.

As Silas toted his gear to pile it beside Whit's, the marshal met him on the way to the chosa. The anger had set hard in Whit's eyes and Silas figured it best to ignore him until he proposed their next move. As he waited, he studied the sun, which had cleared the hillocks and was climbing in a pastel sky. For several seconds, he heard the popping and crackling but it failed to register with him. Then he caught a whiff of pungent smoke and twirled around. Whit had already fired the wickiup and now he was tossing a bundle of smoldering brush onto the grass roof of the chosa.

"Guess we won't be staying the night here again," Silas offered as tongues of flame began to lick at the roof and spew out sparks and smoke. The wickiup whooshed into flames and quickly the chosa was engulfed, the basket of jerky by the wall darkening and finally flaring up.

Whit turned to Silas. "If that red devil Sulky ever looks back, he'll know he'll not sleep here again."

Silas nodded and turned to stare at the sun, not caring to watch the senseless destruction of the brush lodge and chosa. The smoke burned at his eyes until they filled with tears and he wiped them with his bandanna. Grabbing his canteen, he strode to the water hole, wondering all the way if Sulky or Whit were the bigger savage. At the water, he dipped the cloth, squeezing it of the excess liquid, then washed the stinging sensation from his eyes. That done, he filled his canteen.

"Silas," Whit called, "quit lollygagging around. We've a ways to go before high sun."

Turning around, Silas caught another lungful of smoke and through the stinging in his eyes, he saw Whit tying his bedroll, saddlebags and canteen to this saddle. Silas jogged to his gear and did likewise. Whit had that impatient tone in his voice now and he was ready to go. Silas didn't ask questions because for once, he didn't want to know Whit's plan. Whatever it was, it meant but one thing — miles and miles of walking with a heavy load and little water.

When everything was secure, Whit jerked the saddle to his chest, then threw it over his shoulder, wincing under the load until he got it balanced. Bending over, he picked up his carbine and pointed it north. "If you're coming, get a move on it."

"Yeah," Silas answered, "go on. I'll catch up with you." Silas figured Whit was at least twice his own twenty-three years and not near as fit. Silas slipped the canteen strap over his shoulder, put his carbine under his arm and grabbed the saddle, hoisting it to his shoulder and following after Whit who had topped the hill just as he was getting started. Pretty good time for an old fart, Silas thought, but he'd wear down before long.

They walked and Whit always managed to stay ahead, though often by little. Silas took one boring step after another, for a while counting each step to allay the boredom and the agony of his stretched shoulder muscles, of the vindictive sun baking his head and of the burning ground singeing his feet through the soles of his boots. But counting took energy and his load was taking more and more of that so he gave up. He wanted to talk to pass the tedium and the pain, but his bursting lungs wouldn't let him even if Whit would have.

Silas would pause periodically to glance to the south. For an hour, the plume of smoke from the burning house had allowed him to guess the distance he had traveled, but the smoke then dissipated and Silas could only guess. Maybe Whit hadn't burned the dwellings just for spite.

From the chosa, Whit had angled northwest toward the mountains, finally getting into the tall foothills which quickly grew tiresome to climb. Occasionally, Silas would lose Whit when he topped a hill Silas was still climbing. Whit never seemed to stop long enough to do anything but swap the saddle from one hand and shoulder to the other. He was almost inhuman.

About high sun, Silas topped a hill. His eyes were blurry, his knees weak, his back chafed from the load, his lungs bursting for air as he stumbled up the crest and found Whit lying on the ground by his saddle. At first he thought the marshal was dead, but he soon realized Whit was finally resting.

"I pushed you . . ." Whit said, then stopped as Silas dropped down beside him. Suddenly, Whit sounded his shrill whistle as he had done upon waking. Silas wondered how he had the strength for such foolishness.

"I'll be damned," Whit said, raising up from the ground and pointing to the north.

Silas followed the direction of Whit's finger, but his eyes were too blurred to discern anything but more painful miles.

"It's our horses," Whit said.

Rubbing his eyes, Silas stared again and gradually he saw the two horses, one looking toward them, the other pawing at the ground.

Whit whistled again and the nearest horse, maybe a third of a mile away, stumbled forward, then advanced at a slow walk. "I do believe Sulky hobbled them for us."

"Why?" Silas rasped, his dry voice a whisper from want of water.

"So he could get a good start on us. He's at least a half a day ahead of us, maybe more because he's got two horses to switch off on. Sulky figures we can't catch up with him."

If Sulky was that far ahead of them, Silas wondered if they'd ever catch up with the Bastrop gang which was likely a day or more ahead of them. He thought of the reward money hanging on their heads and it no longer seemed so enticing. Zack had been figuring on some reward money too, but now he was beyond money and pain. Silas would trade his share of the money right now for a little less pain and a hot bath, a feather bed and a soft woman to rub the aches out of his exhausted body. He watched Whit reach for his canteen and Silas fumbled for his own, glad the marshal was thirsty again. Silas had taken water only when Whit had, even though it had seemed like forever since he could muster enough spit to spit. He jerked the cork from the canteen neck and measured his swigs with Whit's. The water ran warm but wet down his throat and he savored its dampness, holding for a moment a cheek-bulging mouthful, then letting it trickle down his throat, relishing its tickle. Releasing the canteen spout from his lips and swallowing the rest of the water, he could not help but smile, even though his chapped and cracked lips pained him. He felt the smile melt into a frown as Whit plugged his own canteen and forced himself to his feet.

"You coming, girl?" Whit asked, as he grabbed his saddle and carbine.

At times, Silas had to fight an urge to plug the old fart in the back. He could blame it on the Bastrops, but the hell of it was New Mexico Territory still needed a few crusty old codgers like Whitman to end lawlessness and pave the way for statehood. Silas, though, knew he darn sure didn't need

Whit. Maybe if they did luck out into some reward money, Silas could use his share to find him a respectable job and a little house to live in. He wasn't going to get rich on the sixty dollars a month Whit was paying him.

Silas shoved himself up, surprised that his anger had generated so much energy. Slinging his saddle over his shoulder and picking up his carbine, he lunged forward under the weight, caught his balance, then started down the hill's incline, determined to catch Whit. Halfway down the hill he caught, then passed Whit for the first time since they had left Sulky's blazing chosa. He saw in Whit's gray eyes a flicker of defeat, that while youth might not be wiser than age, it was damn sure stronger. Though he never turned back to watch Whit, Silas felt his pace was stretching the distance between the two.

Finally reaching Whit's chestnut, Silas dropped his gear, fell down upon it and called to his bay. His animal stopped grazing and moved awkwardly toward him. Both horses were hobbled. If Sulky hadn't impeded the horses, he and Whit might never have caught up to them. Were the roles reversed, Silas wondered if Whit would've hobbled a horse for Sulky.

His own horse limped up about the same

time Whit tossed his gear beside Silas. Whit untied his canteen again, uncorked it and drew hard on the water. Silas's mouth burned with envy, but he was feeling a new superiority over Whit and he spurned instinct, deciding he could endure the thirst a little longer.

Whit plugged his canteen and drew the sleeve of his shirt across his lips. "Drink up, Silas," he said. "We can make water by dusk."

"I'll manage," Silas answered, though the raspiness of his voice suggested he wouldn't wait long.

"Suit yourself," the marshal said, approaching his chestnut, and rubbing his sleek neck.

Without waiting for orders, Silas untied the gear on his saddle and arose, lugging his saddle and saddle blanket with him to his bay. Lowering the saddle to the ground, he tossed the blanket easily over his mount's back. Taking a deep breath, he jerked up the saddle and pitched it at the saddle blanket, but he misjudged his strength and his aim. The leather fender and stirrup did not clear the animal's back, striking harmlessly into his side. The animal nickered and twisted around to stare. Silas laughed at his blunder, the first time he'd laughed since

Zack's death. For a moment, he felt giddy and turned to Whit.

"After we get our splits of the reward money, we'll both think this is funny, Whit."

The marshal's gray eyes bore hard into him and Silas realized he'd made another mistake.

"What do you mean, *our* splits of the reward money?" Whit whispered, his brow furrowed.

Silas stiffened and let the saddle slide back to the ground, confusing his horse even more "My split of the reward money?"

Whit crossed his arms over his chest and the badge hidden beneath his vest. "I hired you and you get sixty dollars a month as deputy marshal. The rewards, if Sulky leaves any Bastrops, go to the marshal."

For a moment, Silas doubted the marshal's words, but then he saw the set of Whit's jaw and the hardness in his eyes. Silas picked up his canteen, unplugged it and sucked hard at its contents, wishing all the time it were something stronger.

CHAPTER 6

Sulky slid from Ember, landing softly on the ground, then kneeling by the pile of horse droppings. As he reached to finger the dung, his eyes studied the surrounding earth and his hand froze but a finger's length from the dung. The sign had been growing fresher as surely as the terrain was changing from the pygmy forest of piñon and juniper to the tall pines and now, maybe he had found the freshest of all. Crouching, he stepped over the droppings toward a patch of cliff rose. A brown stub at the plant's base seemed unnatural and when Sulky reached to pick it up, he nodded to himself. It was the remains of a cigarette, still warm. Holding it to his nose, he detected a faint, putrid odor over the tobacco. The man with the rotten teeth had ridden this way. Sulky stuck the nub of a cigarette between his lips and sucked. He despised its taste, but his hollow cheeks sank deeper beneath his cheekbones. Then he exhaled a wisp of smoke before the cigarette crumbled in his mouth. He spit out the tobacco fragments. He was close upon the evil White Eyes. Sulky and Bad Teeth had shared his wife and now a cigarette.

"Bad Teeth," Sulky whispered, "I kill you."

Sulky arose and studied the trail of droppings pointing toward the mountains. The six riders were heading for the high country, but they were fools. The White Man was a weakling outside of his towns and away from his forts. The White Man did not understand nature, could not survive like the Apache, who was at home in the mountains or in the desert.

And the White Man, except maybe Bill Whitman, did not carry vengeance like the Apache. Whitman was aging like himself or Sulky knew he would never have slipped over him back at the chosa and escaped with his horses. Somewhere behind him, Bill Whitman would be following him and by now the marshal would have found his horses. Whitman was too stubborn a man to give up a trail, too mean to wonder where it would lead. He just followed a trail like a wolf on a scent.

Sulky mounted Ember and rode toward the mountains, recalling that at one time

Whitman had been tough, but not mean. He had scouted for Army pay to support his wife and daughter and to save for the Arizona ranch he one day planned to own. Then his family had died a violent death by Apache hands. Whitman went on a two-week drunk and when he sobered up in the Fort Bowie stockade, something in him had died with his family and he meant to take it out on the world.

Whitman had been a good scout, but after that, he was a deadly scout. It had been Whitman who had found him delirious, staggering around the grizzly's carcass, a bloody knife still in his hand, his own blood streaming from the savage wound along his back. Whitman had settled him and used strange medicine on his wound, pouring a bottle of whiskey over his raw flesh. Sulky still remembered it like liquid fire, and the fire smoldered still, even now bothering his shoulder.

Behind him rode Bill Whitman. Sulky knew he must kill the evil White Eyes before Whitman caught up or he might have to fight the marshal. His jaw clenched at the possibility. Maybe he had been foolish to leave Whitman's horses hobbled for him, but Sulky could never forget that Whitman had carried him wounded back to Fort

Bowie where the other Apache scouts had used good medicines to heal him. Whitman had even clipped the grizzly's claws for him and Sulky had used them to make a necklace.

"Easy, Ember," Sulky said, noticing the horse's ears flick forward. Then an antlered buck dashed from a circle of junipers and up a mountain, dotted with pine trees.

He must be cautious now, Sulky knew. He had few bullets for his pistol and rifle, the bad men having stolen his cartridge belt from his wickiup. But an Apache knew many ways to kill. Reaching behind him, Sulky patted the antlered deer head and skin spread out over Ember's rump. When the bad men saw him wearing the antlers, they would remember him.

Pulling his holstered revolver from a belt with empty cartridge loops, Sulky broke open the revolver and examined the cylinder, five chambers holding but hulls, the sixth having his only live round. His thumb over the live round, he held up his pistol and let the hulls fall to the ground. Then he snapped the cylinder back in place and reholstered his Colt .45.

One bullet and six men.

He let the sling around his shoulder slide down his left arm and his hand caught the

78

Henry .44 repeater. Ammunition was low for it as well. The Henry was old, like him, but it was a survivor and he enjoyed the feel of it, reminding him of his days as a warrior. Switching hands, he slid the gun in the crook of his left elbow and jerked the lever, ejecting a bullet at a time into the palm of his left hand. One, two, three, four, five times he caught a bullet. The sixth time the repeater produced only a metallic hiccup.

Six bullets total and six men.

Sulky slowly slid the five .44 caliber rounds back into his Henry. He could use them, if he must, in his revolver, but they were much more valuable and more accurate in his rifle. He still had his knife, though, and thirty arrows for his bow. But his best weapon was his knowledge of this country. He knew things the White Man could never learn. He lifted the sling and slid his left arm beneath it and let the rifle fall to his side.

Nudging Ember with his knee, Sulky glanced over his shoulder to check that Bonita was following. He stared a moment beyond the horse to the east, figuring he had more to fear from Bill Whitman than from the six men ahead, no matter his ammunition shortage. Bill Whitman was as unpredictable as a sidewinder without a rattle.

Ember moved with strong, easy strides. Sulky kept Ember among the dwindling piñon and junipers and the proliferating pines for cover should the riders be watching. Occasionally, he found more sign of the horsemen ahead, a fist-sized rock knocked loose from its earthen cradle by a horse's hoof, trampled groundsel and more horse dung. Sulky studied the wide but shallow valley ahead, remembering that it ran into a narrower valley bisected by a stream. The bad White Eyes would camp by the water, Sulky was sure as he looked up to the high mountains looming beyond, screening the sun and casting a shadow that crawled away from the mountain inch by inch. With maybe an hour or less of good light, Sulky figured he must move faster so he could find his prey and study the one he would kill. He wanted the one who had mutilated his wife with the knife or with the cigarette.

"Bonita," he called and Dawn's mare trotted up to him. He grabbed the halter which he had draped over her neck and started toward the valley, riding at a canter for several minutes. Ember enjoyed the pace and wanted to go faster, but Sulky held him back. Occasionally, as he bounced in his rawhide saddle, Sulky would feel a stab of pain in his shoulder. Would he ever outlive the grizzly's wound? Then Sulky rode into the valley and he could hear the rush of water from the stream. The noise and surprise would be his ally.

Sulky could feel the anticipation of the hunt building within him. It was instinct honed from years on the desert and in the mountains and he pulled up on the reins. He knew his quarry was near. He nudged Ember with his knee and the horse angled toward the hill where the trees were thicker, but Ember was thirsty and smelled the water. He nickered and Bonita tossed her head as they moved up the hill away from the water.

"Later, water I give you," Sulky whispered. "For now, stay silent, Ember. Stay silent, Bonita. I near killers of Dawn."

Briefly, he found a clearing among the pines with plenty of tall grass. He dismounted and quickly cross-hobbled both mounts so they could not wander far from the clearing. The horses blew and snorted and tossed their heads toward the stream, but finally began to graze.

"Sulky return later. Water he give you."

He opted for his Colt, Henry and knife over his bow and arrows and stepped into the trees, advancing along the mountain, its long shadows verging on darkness. Time was running out. He started trotting through the pines, holding his Henry in his left hand and angling down the mountain slope, watching the signs of the White Eyes. It would be good to find them before dark, so he could study them. They had kept a cold camp last night and he doubted they would build a fire tonight. He listened to his measured breath and the fall of his moccasined feet. As he ran, he flushed a stellar jay from a low branch and the bird took up its shrill cry. To an Apache, that cry would mean alarm, but not to the White Eyes. Sulky ran with a gentle breeze at his back and the roar of the rushing stream to his side, remembering how he had run mountains as a youth for fun and later as a young man for survival. He could not outrun a horse, but he could run long and hard, easily outdistancing any white man he had ever encountered. To the Apache, running was survival.

Ahead through the thinning trees his eyes detected movement. He darted to the nearest pine and stopped, hearing as he did the nickering of a horse, then another. The horses had caught his scent on the wind. Sulky clenched his fist. Dawn's killers were near. He waited a moment, until the horses had settled, then peeked around the tree. Between the trees, he could see a lanky man with scraggly hair and beard, pointing his finger and shouting something, as if he were in command. Sulky's jaw went stiff. The man had a cigarette clamped in his mouth.

This was the one Sulky wanted, but he must move closer to study the camp. He stepped away from the tree, then froze at the snap of a twig just down the slope. Half a step beyond the tree, Sulky knew he was visible if someone approached, but he also knew from Apache instinct that sudden movement would be more noticeable than his possible exposure, so he held tight his pose and his breath. He heard footsteps downwind and nearing. Exhaling his breath, slowly he leaned back and pulled himself behind the tree, his hand falling to the pistol with but one cartridge. Tight against the tree, Sulky leaned his head half an eye beyond its trunk and watched.

Not forty paces down the slope, a man with red hair and a patch over his left eye was climbing toward him, slapping the trail dust from his shirt with a greasy hat. He was an ugly man with a shriveled face made homelier by the black eyepatch. He looked mean enough never to have lost a fight and ugly enough never to have walked away unscathed. Knowing that this man had had his wife, Sulky could taste the bitter bile of vengeance.

White Eyes took two more steps, flushing a cottontail rabbit from the bushes. The terrified rabbit darted up the hill toward Sulky's tree, coming close enough for Sulky to kick him, then darting away in the opposite direction. An Apache would know that something was amiss by the erratic change in the rabbit's course, but not this white man. He stopped a dozen paces from Sulky, replaced his hat and turned his back upslope to take a leak. Sulky wanted to spring down the mountain upon him and kill him with his bare hands; but he fought against the impulse throbbing within him for it might warn the others.

The red-haired man was slow attending his business. As Sulky heard him make water, his gaze fell upon the knife scabbard on One Eye's cartridge belt. From behind, the scabbard looked damaged and Sulky wondered if this were the man who had mutilated his wife with a knife. The bile of revenge grew ranker in his mouth. Had he brought his bow and arrows, Sulky would kill One Eye right now because he could do it quietly. Sulky pulled all of his head behind the tree now and felt his lips tighten across his clenched teeth. Dawn had meant more to him than he had ever realized. She was all he had had.

Tonight, Sulky would kill One Eye!

He leaned against the tree, angry that he must wait for revenge. Then he heard One Eye gradually making his way back down the slope. After giving One Eye plenty of time to reach camp, Sulky began a cautious ascent from tree to tree, going as quickly as he dared because little light remained. Then he heard voices over the rushing waters. He dropped to his knees, slid to his belly and crawled to a boulder outcrop. Lifting his head, he studied the camp through a vee between two boulders.

Bedrolls, six of them, were laid out in a circle. One Eye was lounging on the one farthest from him and nearest the stream and the horses. He would be the most difficult to reach in the night, but Sulky would try. Bad Teeth prowled from bedroll to bedroll, smoking another cigarette. On another bedroll, a man sat reading a book to a youth with a funny, almost childish look about him. A fifth man was tending the horses and the last seemed already asleep.

The man holding the book read until darkness was upon them and then he was quiet. Sulky heard one of them arguing about money with Bad Teeth, the one that seemed to be the leader.

"Who's in charge here?" Sulky heard Bad Teeth ask.

"You are, Ben," another grumbled, "but we'd feel a lot better if you'd split the money or rotate the watches at night."

"What about the watches?"

"Hell, Ben," the same voice griped, "you know first watch is best cause you don't get waked in the middle of your sleep."

"Okay, dammit, Leander," Ben spit out. "We'll rotate the damn watches, just you bastards don't be asleep when Whit Whitman rides up. Prentice, you take first watch."

They feared Bill Whitman, too, Sulky thought as he craned his neck to see One Eye stand up from his bedroll, mumbling something that was washed out by the distance and the sound of the stream.

"No matter to me, boys," Ben shouted. "Just remember you'd be nothing without me to look out for you."

"Dummy'd do just as good," one of them called out, drawing a couple of laughs.

Sulky watched the sinister shadow that seemed to be One Eye pick up what looked like a carbine and head back down the trail.

Sulky dropped his head, glad that One Eye would take the first watch. Though his heart raced with revenge, Sulky decided not to risk stalking One Eye during his watch, but to wait until One Eye returned for sleep. Sulky had many nights before crawled among enemy camps and he relished the thrill.

He sat up and leaned his back against one of the boulders, then propped his Henry against the rock. He would leave it here while he slipped into the camp. If he were discovered, he could race back here for cover and use ammunition enough to knock off one or two before making a run for it. Waiting, Sulky watched a fingernail of a moon climb the sky, casting off enough light that he could discern the dark shapes on the ground below him. Not since he had helped find Geronimo had Sulky spent a night like this, stalking men and wondering if he'd see tomorrow's sunrise.

Closing his eyes, Sulky could see Dawn and it pained him that he had left her without Bonita to ride away from these evil men. He regretted ever seeing that white deer, even if its hide would have made a fine robe for his son. The Apache understood the value of sons because they were so hard to come by. The White Man was as prolific as bees and could never value a son. Now because of white men, he could never have a son. He was alone in the world. He opened his eyes as if it all might be a horrible dream, but he saw the crescent moon, frowning down upon him. He sat with his loneliness until he heard movement in the camp and the voice of One Eye waking his replacement. Leaning forward into a crouch, Sulky watched the new guard stumble back down the trail as One Eye crawled under his blanket. The air was cool now and Sulky's skin prickled from the slight breeze and the great anticipation. He must wait for One Eye to sleep.

His hand slipped to his revolver and then to his other side, patting the knife in its scabbard. He breathed deeply, letting the air out slowly, quietly. The task was before him now. He crawled from behind the rocks, then froze a moment, then inched forward again, then turned still again. Creep and freeze, creep and freeze. He had done it thousands of times as a game as a child and later as a scout, slipping unobserved into and out of enemy camps. Progress was slow, but stealth was safer. Sulky inched closer to the sleeping men, halting even his breath when the horses neighed. They had caught his scent or heard him and a couple pawed at the ground and blew.

He waited and waited, making no sudden movements to startle the horses, and then he crept forward again, even slower and finally he neared the camp perimeter, pulling out his knife as he reached the first bedroll. The breath of the nearest man was heavy, but the one beyond him was restless and turned suddenly in his blanket. Sulky leaned quickly into the ground and held his breath, but the man must be having a fitful dream. Sulky squirmed ahead, crawling inside the circle of bedrolls.

One Eye was closer and Sulky could feel the hate heating his blood. He wanted to jump up and attack, waking every one so they would know that it was Dawn's husband who would terrorize them until they all were dead. One Eye would never know, but Sulky would reveal himself to the others come morning. Then he moved beside One Eye, a horse snorting at him. He lay still, counting One Eye's breaths. They would be among his last.

Sulky studied his quarry and inched his knife hand closer to One Eye's neck, his fingers scraping against the ground and then against the knife scabbard at One Eye's side. Leaving his own knife on the ground, he pulled softly on One Eye's, the scabbard moving with it.

One Eye shifted his arm. Sulky froze. One Eye turned over. Sulky fought the instinct to move for his pistol and shoot One Eye. One Eye shifted again, this time his hand coming to rest on the ground close to Sulky's knife. Sulky swallowed a breath of relief that One Eye had not touched him and waited, lifeless as a rock. Finally, he reached with both hands for One Eye's knife, holding the scabbard with one hand and slowly, gently sliding the knife free with the other.

One Eye groaned a moment in his sleep. Sulky knew he should kill One Eye now, but he burned to know if One Eye was the man who had mutilated his wife. Holding One Eye's knife with one hand, he grabbed the blade between his thumb and forefinger and slid them toward the point. Razor sharp, the knife blade was bent, then split a hair from the tip.

This was the one. Sulky felt a cruel satisfaction coursing through his veins as he rolled a fraction closer to his quarry, then lifted One Eye's knife. He would kill this evil man with his own knife.

But behind him, he heard footsteps. The guard! Had he seen something? Was he returning to switch off? Sulky dropped his hand, his fingers brushing against One Eye's hand. Sulky wanted to twist his head to watch the guard, but feared the slightest movement might give himself away. He waited, knowing his eyes had grown accustomed to the moon's dim light, but hoping the guard's eyesight was not as sharp. The man stopped at a nearby blanket and bent down for something. Then Sulky heard the guard unplug his canteen and take a drink. So like the White Man, Sulky thought, to return for his canteen when the sweet water from the stream was available and so much better. The guard swallowed hard, relishing the water, then capped his canteen and dropped it on his bedroll, the clatter disturbing the horses. The guard ambled back down the trail.

Sulky waited. Finally, satisfied the guard was a good distance away, he rose to his knees, One Eye's knife still in his hand. Then in one sudden, fluid motion, his left hand flew to One Eye's mouth and his right hand took revenge for Dawn.

CHAPTER 7

Hearing the others stirring, Dummy relaxed his fingers on his pistol grip and let his eyelids crack to see the daylight. His gun-hand trembled, but not from the cool, damp fog enveloping the mountain. He took to snapping his finger, still frightened from the strange night noises.

With his right hand, he rubbed the lingering sleep from his eyes, his snapping finger offering a steady beat from his left palm. He propped himself up on an elbow and looked around. The heavy fog distorted things so that the others seemed like ghosts as they pulled on their boots and gathered their bedrolls. The fog had coated the grass with a heavy dew which hung in teardrops from every plant stem, leaf and blade until they fell upon the earth. Bastrop was up, prowling around like a she bear guarding her cubs and twice as touchy.

Behind him, Dummy heard a splash of

water and then a loud yell. His finger snapped faster as he twisted to watch Claude throwing handfuls of the cold water on his face and shouting from the wet shock. Dummy sighed, relieved that it was only Claude. Claude was too big to be scared of anything and Dummy felt safer knowing he was nearby, especially after last night. Even now with it light, the jitters were still crawling up Dummy's back like a nest of roaches.

Last night when he had been the scaredest, when he had held his breath for fear it might reveal him to some unseen evil, when he had lain as stiff as a board, he had wanted to cry for help. But the evil out there might have heard him and killed him. And if there was no evil, the others would laugh at him and curse him for disturbing their rest. His finger was still snapping when he heard footsteps approaching. He sat up, those roaches still slithering up his back, and faced Pete, who always tended the horses first in the morning and then helped Dummy gather his belongings for another day of hard riding. Dummy straightened up, encouraged by Pete's smile.

Pete spoke. "You're jumpy this morning."

Dummy shrugged. It would be too difficult to explain and the others might overhear his words and laugh at him.

Pete, standing over him in his rain slicker, patted Dummy on the shoulder. "It's okay now. Nights are sometimes spooky, especially when you're on the run," he said with regret in his tone. Motioning for Dummy to hold out his hand, Pete dropped several chunks of dried apple into his open palm. Pete always saw that Dummy got his share of food.

Dummy shoved a piece in his mouth, then remembered the manners his mother had taught him. "Thanks, Pete," he mumbled over the apple's sweetness.

"Finish up, then roll up your blankets. I've saddled your horse and Ben's getting restless."

Nodding, Dummy grinned, but the smile turned sour at the shout of Ben Bastrop.

"Everybody up," Bastrop yelled.

Dummy looked around. Everyone had arisen, except Prentice — but nobody moved to rouse him — and himself.

"Fog like this," Bastrop started, spitting his cigarette out and throwing his chest forward like he enjoyed being in command, "I figure we can build us a fire, make a little coffee and fry a little saltpork. Nobody'll spot the smoke. A little breakfast would do us good."

Pete stepped warily toward Bastrop. "Fine, as long as you send someone besides Dummy for wood."

"Yeah," Leander said, moving into camp from the horses, "as long as you're keeping our share of the train money, I'm not doing any chores for you." Leander's green eyes, soft except when he spoke of money, were hard, Dummy thought.

Claude moved in between Pete and Leander, not saying a thing, but fingering the bearclaw necklace around his neck and nodding, leaving no doubt that he agreed with Pete and Leander.

"Why don't you have Prentice fetch your wood and boil your coffee and fry your bacon," Leander challenged.

Bastrop's chest sank. "You keep forgettin' who's boss here, Leander. I make the decisions."

Leander chuckled, "Dummy could make all the decisions you've made. Get up and ride, outrun Whit Whitman, stay together, we're safer in numbers. Why don't you make a tough decision and get Prentice up off his lazy butt?"

His right hand clenching into a fist, Bastrop pounded it into his left palm. "I'm the boss, Leander, and don't you and the others forget it. Dammit, it's your fault he's not up."

Leander stepped toward Bastrop. "How's that?"

"Demanding we change the rotation on guards, that's how," Bastrop said, pounding his fist into his palm again, a cynical smile exposing his brown, rotting teeth. "We were all used to the rotation until we changed it."

A grin creased Leander's face, then erupted into a throaty laugh that resembled a growl. "The rest of us are up, Ben. Now if you're the leader, get Prentice up and let him nursemaid you."

Bastrop clenched both fists and swallowed hard. "You'll regret this, Leander."

"Not as much as you will, Ben," Leander sneered, "if Prentice is in a bad mood."

Dummy stared at Bastrop. Nobody'd stood up to him like this before and his face was flushed red with rage. Bastrop took a tentative step to Prentice's blanket, then a more confident step as his hand fell to his sidearm.

"Prentice," he yelled, "get your lazy butt up and fetch us some firewood. The boys've decided they want breakfast."

Prentice, to Dummy's surprise, never moved. He was turned on his side, his bony shoulder poking up under the wool blanket which reached his ears, his head strangely fixed beneath the blanket.

"Dammit, Prentice," Bastrop shouted. "Quit possumin' and do what I say. I'm the boss around here."

Still, Prentice didn't move. Dummy, his mouth full of his last bit of apple, stood up in case trouble resulted.

Bastrop moved a step closer until he stood over Prentice. Cautiously, Bastrop toed Prentice with his boot. "Prentice," he said, his voice softer. "Prentice?"

Now Dummy realized something was wrong. He'd never heard Bastrop speak so softly.

With the heel of his boot, Bastrop shoved hard against Prentice's shoulder. Then he jumped back and Dummy gasped, almost sucking the bite of apple down in his throat.

Prentice's shoulder tumbled slowly over, pulling the blanket with it. Everything rolled over. Except Prentice's head.

Dummy would have screamed, except for the apple caught in his throat and he gasped for breath, for a moment uncertain if the apple he had already eaten would stay down.

"Cut his damn head off, somebody did," Bastrop called, as if the others needed a description. Then he laughed, low at first, then louder until it seemed to echo off the mountains.

There was an evil in these mountains, Dummy thought, still fighting the nausea in his stomach. It was too horrible to look at Prentice, but Dummy was too curious not to. He covered his eyes with his hand, then peeked between his fingers.

Feeling a soothing hand on his shoulder, he looked up from behind his fingers to see Pete smiling at him.

"You okay, Dummy?"

Dummy nodded, casting a final glance toward Prentice as Leander pushed Bastrop aside to pull the blanket over the torso, then the severed head. Dummy wanted to get away so he grabbed his shoes and slipped them on. They were loose without laces, but he didn't care because the laces were always difficult to tie. He wanted to leave, but where could he hide from this evil?

Bastrop finally stopped laughing. "What about breakfast?" he asked.

"What about Prentice?" Claude said to no one in particular.

"Nah," said Leander, "we'd have to gut and skin him first."

Everyone, even Pete, laughed, though Dummy didn't understand why. He felt sick and wanted to get away from the awful sight that was burned in his brain.

He retreated from Pete, who reached out for him and grabbed his hand. Pete's grasp was friendly, not threatening, but Dummy shook himself free, stumbling over his blanket.

"Wait Dummy, let me get you something," Pete commanded and Dummy stopped, knowing he could trust Pete but not so certain as Pete moved to Prentice's saddle, lying on the ground within reach of the dead man. Pete untied a dirty slicker from the saddle laces and returned to Dummy with it.

"This'll protect you from the wet," Pete said, offering the slicker to Dummy.

Taking a step back, Dummy shook his head. He wanted a slicker, but not that one, not the one of a dead man. He fumbled in his mind for an explanation so not to hurt Pete's feelings, but the most his tongue could muster was a hard word. "No," he said, and it came out louder than he meant for it to.

Pete smiled and pulled the slicker back. "I understand, Dummy. Here's what we'll do. You need a slicker."

As Dummy stared, uncertain what his friend meant to do, Pete took off his own slicker and tossed it toward him. Dummy caught it and felt a smile sliding along his lips. He got a sleeve tangled as he tried to put it on, fighting against the oilskin and grinning broadly when he finally slipped into it. It was a little big, but he'd grow to it, he knew. Now, he had his own gun and his own slicker. "Thanks, Pete," Dummy said.

Pete just nodded. "If you walk a bit, don't go far. You could get lost in this fog. You keep where you can see one of us or the horses because this killer could still be out here."

Dummy took a step away, then answered, "Yeah." Dummy moved a step at a time, stopping after each one, turning and checking that he could see camp. After maybe twenty steps — he wasn't sure because counting was so hard — he could just make out their ghostly forms moving in the distance. But though he could barely see them, their voices carried loudly through the fog.

"Leander, you know so much," Bastrop said, "was this Whit Whitman's doings?"

Pete said, "It's gotta be that Indian we saw as we left the woman."

Dummy shivered and wanted to go deeper into the fog where he couldn't hear them. Fear was an itch he could never scratch enough to lose.

"We gonna bury him?" Claude asked.

"Did you bring a shovel, Claude?" Ben answered, his voice booming through the fog.

"Nope," Claude admitted.

"Then we're not gonna do nothing," Ben said. "I'd hate to be here scratching a grave out of the ground with my fingernails when Whit Whitman showed up. Where you going, Pete?"

Dummy saw one of the men move away from the others, then heard Pete's voice. "To get my Bible, we at least owe him that."

Shortly, Dummy saw Pete's hazy figure return to the others. It took Pete a moment to find a passage among the Bible's hard words. Dummy wished he could figure out the letters on those pages, hundreds of them, but he just couldn't make sense of them in his mind, much less pronounce them as well as Pete did.

Then Pete's voice came reassuringly through the fog. "This is from the third chapter of Ecclesiastes," he paused and there was a stirring among the others as they coughed and cleared their throats.

Pete read. " 'God shall judge the righteous and the wicked, for there is a time there for every purpose and for every work.' "

Dummy didn't understand it, but the

101

words were pretty the way Pete read them so well.

" 'I said in mine heart concerning the estate of the sons of men that God might manifest them and that they might see that they themselves are beasts.

" 'For that which befalleth the sons of men befalleth beasts; even one thing befalleth them: as the one dieth, so dieth the other; yea, they have all one breath; so that a man hath no preeminence above a beast: for all is vanity.' "

Dummy wasn't sure what vanity was and he was confused about men and the beasts. Perplexed, he turned away from the men and faced the fog, Pete's voice continuing behind him.

" 'All go unto one place: all are of the dust, and all turn to dust again.

" 'Who knoweth the spirit of man that goeth upward and the spirit of the beast that goeth downward to the earth?

" 'Wherefore I perceive that there is nothing better than that a man should rejoice in his own works; for that is his portion: for who shall bring him to see what shall be after him?' "

"Amen," Pete said and Dummy knew it was over.

"What the hell did that mean, Pete?" Ben

102

Bastrop's voice sounded loud and threatening. "Man and beasts? Hell of a thing to read at a man's funeral."

Dummy took a step deeper into the fog, then realized he might get lost so he backed up a step, staring into the fog, wishing Bastrop wouldn't criticize Pete's reading. Dummy worried that the fog was hiding the beast that had killed Prentice and he took to snapping his finger. He wished for the sun to clear the fog so he could leave this place with the others.

Then his fear took shape out of the fog, at first something as indefinite as a log, seeming to loom out of the mist, and the log turned into a horse and it came slowly toward him, Dummy thinking at first it was an apparition because it advanced on feathery feet without making a noise. And then a twig snapped.

Dummy's finger twitched faster against his palm. He blinked his eyes once, twice, three times so the form would come into shape. The horse appeared to be carrying a tree with tiny branches atop it. The horse moved closer.

Terror stabbed at Dummy's brain. It wasn't a tree, but a deer. He could see its antlers now and the fur of its head — the deer on horseback that they had seen after hurting the woman. Dummy's mind seemed to trip over itself. He didn't know what to do and then panic took over, but his feet seemed rooted to the ground and he could not run, his tongue seemed stuck to the bottom of his mouth and he could not scream. Opening his mouth, he tried to shout, but nothing but his breath came out. The others would laugh at him for screaming.

But the horse and rider seemed not to see him, even though they were headed right for him. He must protect himself. He fumbled to open his slicker and get his gun. The deer on horseback did not notice him. Dummy felt his hand on the cold metal of his revolver and he tugged on it, but it was stuck in his britches. He tugged again and a third time before it came free. The horse whinnied at the noise but the deer was fearless. Dummy held up the gun, knowing it lacked a trigger and bullets, but feeling safer anyway. His finger slipped into the trigger guard and pulled hard against it.

His brain whirred through its own haze and suddenly his tongue came unstuck.

"Bang!" Dummy screamed. "Bang! Bang!" He screamed louder. The deer on horseback turned sideways and Dummy aimed at the horse. "Bang! Bang!"

Behind him, Dummy heard the rush of

footsteps and then the explosion of live ammunition, the bullets whizzing over his shoulder toward the strange rider.

"Duck, Dummy, duck," he heard Pete yelling, over the gunfire.

But Pete was wrong, Dummy thought. It wasn't a duck, it was a deer. "Bang! Bang!," Dummy yelled, pulling tightly against the trigger guard. He fired again but his aim was knocked awry by a blinding jolt from behind. He felt himself falling forward through the air as if he were flying and then he crashed into the ground in a heap, heavy weight briefly upon him, then jumping up. Dummy heard the explosion of a gun overhead. It was Pete, but he didn't understand why Pete had shoved him to the ground.

More bullets rang out behind him and Dummy turned over and pushed himself up on his hands and knees. Pete, kneeling beside him, knocked him down again and squeezed off another shot. Then Dummy realized Pete was keeping him out of the line of fire. Dummy was thankful for Pete.

As suddenly as it had started, the firing stopped and all was quiet for a moment. Then from somewhere in the fog, a terrible shriek came from the throat of something living, man or beast Dummy could not tell, but he cringed at the sound as if something had had its throat slit. He remembered Prentice and thought maybe it was his ghost and then he thought of the deer on horseback, but a deer didn't make such horrible noises. It came again from out there somewhere wailing like an angered spirit. And as the screaming trailed off, it was followed by the sounds of galloping hoofbeats seeming to head in the direction they would be going. It had to be the deer on horseback. Dummy wanted to cry, but the others were near and though he didn't care if they saw him cry — because they made fun of him for things far less serious — he didn't want Pete to think him a baby.

"It's okay now, Dummy," Pete said, his calm voice as smooth as silk. "He's gone."

Dummy wasn't so sure things were safe because he heard footsteps. Cautiously getting to his knees, he saw Ben Bastrop jogging toward him.

"Anybody hurt here?" Bastrop called out.

Figuring Bastrop was more curious than concerned, Dummy got up on his feet, brushing his new slicker off, and let Pete answer.

"No wounds," Pete said.

"It's that damn Injun we saw, wasn't it."

Dummy knew it wasn't an Indian, but that deer. He wanted to tell Ben that, but the words were stuck in his brain and when he dislodged them, they came not in orderly sentences, but in an avalanche of disjointed letters which started his tongue to spouting strange sounds that made Dummy ashamed.

"First thing Dummy's said that I agree with," Bastrop said, laughing.

And Dummy dropped his head, ashamed that he had tried to explain that it was an evil deer, not an Indian, that had attacked them.

"It's probably an Apache, a few Apaches still roam this country," Pete said.

Dummy bit his lip. He couldn't believe Pete was taking Ben's side that it was an Indian.

"Reckon that was his woman we . . . ?" Bastrop asked, his words trailing into a void Dummy couldn't understand. Bastrop shook his head, spit at the ground and pulled out the makings for another cigarette from his shirt. Adroitly, he took a cigarette paper, dumped a pinch of pouch tobacco on it, folded it, twisting its ends, with one hand and jammed it in his mouth.

"Damn, if we don't have hell to pay. Whit Whitman on our tail and a crazy Apache up ahead of us," he said.

CHAPTER 8

Loathe to leave a meal, the coyote glanced warily over his shoulder, trotting toward the stream, his tail parallel to the ground. Then hiding among the rocks and undergrowth by the water, the coyote peeked at the two approaching riders.

Silas had spotted the coyote first. Though Whit would never have admitted that, Silas had observed that the marshal would rise in his stirrups slightly when he first noticed something, then sink back into his saddle. It was one of the quirks a man picked up about another when they spent time on the trail together and Silas had spotted the coyote before Whit straightened in his saddle. Silas couldn't figure the kill so he studied the coyote which glanced between the carrion and them. Maybe the coyote recognized Whit as kin because nothing but a coyote would cut his deputy out of any reward money. That would make Whit the granddaddy of all coyotes, Silas figured.

Whit reined up and Silas, accustomed to following Whit's lead, did the same. As he stared at the ground the coyote had abandoned, Whit rested one hand atop the other on the saddle horn. "What do you make of it, Silas?"

Silas shifted in his saddle. Damn Whit! He never said what he thought, preferring to make a fool of his deputy first. Silas took a deep breath and thought for a moment, not wanting to admit he hadn't figured the kill. "I'd say that coyote was reluctant to give ground."

Shaking his head like a schoolmarm correcting a wrong answer, Whit cleared his throat and spit the result to the ground. "That wasn't a damn coyote, that was a gray wolf."

Like hell, Silas thought. How could that old fart tell a wolf from a coyote at a distance of seventy-five yards, maybe more? "Looked like a coyote to me, Whit."

"Coloring's about the same, but a coyote runs with his tail between his legs," Whit said. "That animal carried its tail when it trotted off, so it's a gray wolf."

Silas knew not to argue. Whit never spoke unless he was certain of his information. What the hell difference it made was beyond

Silas, but it was the first conversation he'd had with Whit for several miles so there was some benefit in it. "What you figure, Whit?" Silas finally asked, knowing that Whit had already made things out or he wouldn't have asked to begin with.

Taking off his hat, Whit ran his hand through his gray hair. "I'd say Sulky caught up with the Bastrop gang." With the sleeve of his plaid shirt, Whit wiped his brow at the line separating the pale white flesh where his hat rode from the skin darkened from years of riding under an unforgiving southwestern sun. Replacing his hat, Whit shook his reins and the chestnut headed toward the stream and the spot the gray wolf still watched.

Letting the marshal take a good lead, Silas finally nudged his horse into Whit's wake. As he rode, Silas stared at the lump on the ground ahead. Now that Whit had voiced his suspicions, it was evident that it was a corpse. Silas felt icily cold at the thought of another body. That was what bothered him about law enforcement. Seeing Zack get killed, then having to bury him on the trail in an unmarked grave dug with a tin plate was had enough. Then there was Sulky's woman and now this.

Nearing the body, Silas could see it had

been mauled by the wolf. It wasn't a pretty sight and Silas wondered if the queasiness in his stomach would ever go away. Whit seemed as placid as ever.

Reaching the body first, Whit pulled up his horse. "Sulky's up to his old tricks again," he said.

Reining in beside Whit, Silas shrugged. "How's that?"

"He cut his damn head off."

Sure enough, Whit was right. Silas stared at the body, then at the head, a couple of feet away. He hadn't believed Whit's tale about Sulky dumping the heads of his brother and uncle on the parade ground at Fort Bowie. Now he did.

"Hellfire and brimstone, if Sulky didn't take a chunk out of our reward money," Whit said, dismounting and stepping to the disjointed head.

"Your reward money, you mean," Silas said, but Whit ignored the bitterness in his words.

Whit toed the head with his boot, then squinted as it rolled over. Whit squirted a stream of tobacco on the ground. He shook his head. "There goes a good three hundred dollars. This here's Prentice Jones, Prent Jones, One-eyed Prent. Maybe the most dangerous one of them all. Good with a gun, good with a knife."

"Glad he's gone to his grave, then," Silas answered.

"He's not gone to his grave unless you plan on digging him one," Whit answered. "He's gone straight to hell."

"How'd Sulky separate him from the rest?"

Whit stepped back and surveyed the ground around the corpse, lying on a blood-stained blanket. "He didn't."

Silas detected a touch of admiration in Whit's voice.

"See the grass, patches where it's tamped down? They slept here. Sulky slipped in amongst them and gave ol' Prent a haircut down to his neck."

Remembering he had spent a night with Sulky, Silas felt a tightness in his throat.

"This means we'll have to arrest Sulky for murder, take him back for trial."

Silas scratched his chin at Whit's words. They seemed to be laced with a sinister pleasure. "Why?"

Whit screwed up his face and twisted his lips at Silas's intemperate question. His gray eyes had a steelish glint as they clashed with Silas's, but the deputy felt a new mettle in his resolve and he didn't back down. The marshal averted his eyes to his vest pocket and retrieved his tobacco plug and pocket knife.

Glaring down on Whit from his mount, Silas enjoyed the marshal's sudden discomfort. "Why?" he repeated.

"It's the law, Silas," Whit said, his hard eyes narrowing.

"If you'd killed him, you wouldn't be tried," Silas said.

"I'm the law," Whit said, then tossed back his head and dropped some tobacco shavings in his mouth. "It's eighteen-ninety-two, Silas. New Mexico won't become a civilized territory until we stop people from taking the law into their own hands. Hellfire and brimstone, Silas, I hired you to enforce the law, not question it."

Whit was angering. Silas could hear it in his strained voice and see it in the jaw which worked the tobacco hard. Still, Silas thought he had the marshal on the run, like a coyote with his tail between his legs. "Seems the law's harder to figure than I thought."

"A lot of things are harder than you're capable of figuring, deputy." Whit shoved his plug and knife in his vest pocket, then brushed the vest back from his right breast so his tarnished badge appeared. "I've put a lot of miles on this badge, Silas," he said. Then he pointed at Silas's badge. "Yours shines with your lack of experience. Don't forget you're wearing it because I hired you. If you want monthly pay, then don't he getting uppity with me. I'm the law."

Silas acquiesced to the marshal's warning with a nod, but feeling with each bob of his head that he'd triumphed over Whit for once.

"Now, deputy," Whit said, reminding Silas just who was in charge, "let's see if you're smart enough to figure how far behind the Bastrop gang we are."

Here Whit went again, going to give him a lesson in trailing and embarrass him at the same time, Silas thought. He glanced up at the sun, gauging it at its peak, then dismounted and walked around the camp, avoiding the body as much as possible. He could see the grass crushed from five bedrolls now removed and he could even make out what he thought was the trail where Sulky had crawled into camp, but he was uncertain whether it was yesterday or this morning. A man familiar with death on the trail could have told by the decomposition of the body, but Silas wasn't that proficient in scouting and didn't know if he ever cared to be. Striding toward the stream, he found where the horses had been staked. The grass was well trampled and the ground littered with droppings. Silas squatted beside a knot of dung and picked it up, breaking it apart in his hand. It was soft, though not warm, and it held together as he split it. The Bastrop gang had broken camp this morning. Dropping the manure back on the ground, he brushed his hands off against one another and arose to face Whit.

"Maybe five hours, no more behind them," Silas said with all the confidence he could muster.

Whit nodded.

Silas sighed, but it was unlike Whit to give in so easy without making a point. Then Whit spat out a stream of tobacco juice and Silas knew the marshal had a point to make.

"Whenever I'm trailing, deputy," Whit said, "I generally try to figure things out without having to handle horse turds."

Damn him, Silas thought, always enjoying other people's mistakes as if he didn't make any of his own. Silas strode to the stream and bent over to wash the odor from his hands, but there wasn't enough water in all of New Mexico to wash away his growing hate for Whit Whitman. The water was cold, stinging his hands, but he preferred it to Whit's icy words. Finally, when his hands tingled with the cold, he rose slowly, shaking them of their wetness. He turned around to see Whit still watching him.

Motioning to Silas, Whit bent down beside a pair of hoofprints in the grass. "Come here, Silas," he said, "and I'll show you how to tell without getting your hands filthy."

Silas sidled over to Whit and bent down, resting his palms on his knees and studying the hoofprints beneath the marshal's hand.

"On the trail, nature'll give you most of the clues you need if only you're smart enough to put it all together," Whit said. "Now what made this morning different from the others lately?"

Dammit, here it came again, another of Whit's infernal questions. "Fog," Silas answered.

"Right," Whit replied, "but the fog's not as important as what it brought with it."

"A heavy dew?"

"Now you're thinking, Silas. Look at these tracks. The sun's dried them out, but the dew left its mark. You spot it?"

Bending down closer, Silas studied the crumpled blades of grass. He couldn't see much, except bits of dirt clinging to some of the grass. "Nothing except the dirt."

Whit shrugged. "It's right there before your eyes. You're seeing it, but not understanding. The specks of dirt stuck to the wet grass and clung to it after the dew burned away."

Silas looked over his shoulder at the stream, scratched his chin. "Tell me, Whit, how can you be so sure it was dew instead of the horses watering and then tracking up the grass with wet hooves?"

"Intuition, Silas," Whit answered smugly. "We'll follow the tracks out until you're satisfied that it's the dew. Let's fill our canteens, first."

Silas followed Whit to the stream where their horses had wandered to drink. Retrieving his canteen from his saddle, he unplugged it and emptied it into the fast running water. Then he stepped upstream from where the horses were muddying the water and dropped his canteen among the rocks which made the rippling water sing with a rush. The canteen floated the length of its strap, then bobbed a time or two before its neck went under once, twice, three times, in each instance the neck rising not quite as high as it had before. Then it sank and Silas pulled it in as it tugged against the water like a skillet-sized bass against a line. Silas sampled his catch and the water was cool and sweet, then dropped the canteen back in the stream to refill. The water was refreshing and it had felt good all the way down, but it didn't soothe the gnawing in his gut, the craving for a good meal. Tempted to purloin a strip of jerky from his saddlebag and enjoy it while Whit wasn't looking, Silas shrugged off the thought. He wouldn't eat until Whit did or the marshal might think him weak. And Silas was fed up with fulfilling the marshal's expectations.

"You ready," Whit called.

Silas turned around to see Whit already mounted and standing in his stirrups like he always did when he noticed something. Plugging his canteen, Silas grabbed his hay's reins and led him out of the water. As he tied the canteen in place, Whit's chestnut trotted by with Whit preoccupied with what he had spotted. Mounting quickly, Silas clucked his tongue and his hay took out after Whit, but the marshal stopped not twenty yards away and studied the ground, until Silas caught up with him. The marshal nodded to himself.

"Looks like the Bastrops wasted some ammunition on Sulky," Whit said, pointing to the ground.

Following Whit's hand with his eyes, Silas saw several empty cartridge hulls scattered about on the grass. How had the marshal seen them from the stream? Was it his damn intuition he was so proud of? "Think they hit him?"

"Silas, you don't understand Sulky. He's a ghost of a man. You don't see Sulky unless he wants you to see him."

"Wish their aim had been that bad when they bushwhacked us and got Zack," Silas said softly, more to himself than Whit.

"I kinda do myself," Whit answered.

Damn him for never admitting he cared about anybody or anything except his own hide, Silas thought.

"We best move on, Silas. Let's pick up the trail and we'll check the tracks however far away from the stream you want and I'll prove to you it was the dew that left the dirtied grass, not a wet hoof."

Silas grimaced. He had hoped Whit had forgotten about the tracks, but it was human to have a memory lapse and the marshal was inhuman. They rode away, Silas silent and determined not to mention the tracks again.

Whit twisted around in his saddle and stared back at the body. "So long, Prent," he called, "you're with your own kind now, the worms and maggots." Shortly, he pulled up on his reins and Silas's mount sidled in beside the marshal's. "Get down and take a look at the tracks, Silas."

Catching a growl in his throat before it escaped, Silas slid from his saddle and landed hard on the ground. He bent and studied the shallow impression of a horse hoof and the tramped grass imbedded in the imprint. Sure enough, the dirt still clung to this grass. He nodded.

"Like I said, nature gives you all the clues you need as long as you know how to read them," the marshal intoned while Silas remounted.

Then they moved upstream, deeper into the mountains and into the tall timber, riding silently, giving Silas time to cogitate on the life of a lawman and on the mystery that was Whit Whitman. Silas couldn't figure why Whitman was interested in taking Sulky back for trial. It didn't make sense. Why, Sulky probably deserved a proclamation from the territorial governor for his close shave of Prent Jones.

Silas was shocked when Whit Whitman spoke because it seemed as if the marshal had been reading his mind as closely as he read the trail they were following.

"I would've been a different man, had it not been for Sulky," he said, then said nothing more.

It wasn't an apology, Silas figured, and if it were an admission, Silas didn't know of what, but it gave him something to think about instead of his saddle weariness and his hollow stomach.

CHAPTER 9

The mountain air, fresh and cool, tickled
his lungs as Dummy studied the pines. He
had never seen so many trees and towering
ahead was the peak the others called White
Mountain. But White Mountain was green
two-thirds of its imposing height and a barren blue the top third, not white. He didn't
understand that, but most things he
couldn't comprehend didn't bother him.
The deer on horseback, though, was different. Dummy just couldn't figure how the
deer had learned to ride or how he handled
the reins, much less how he had held a knife
to cut off Prentice's head. He shuddered
and wished the others, circled on their
horses and gesturing wildly at each other,
would finish their argument. Though he had
questions about the deer on horseback, he
didn't want to tarry in case the deer was
looking for them again. And most of all, he

dreaded nightfall when the deer might return.

"Dammit," Ben Bastrop said, "this is what
we'll do."

They were talking about the deer on
horseback as they had since morning and it
frightened Dummy.

"He's bound to have fallen back in behind
us," Bastrop said.

Leander spit out a challenge. "Ben, you
don't know where in tarnation he is!"

Ben, a cigarette hanging out of the corner
of his mouth, blew smoke at Leander.
"Then where in hell do you think he is?"

"Ahead of us. Why slip in behind and trail
us when he knows the direction we're heading? He was riding this way when we shot
at him," Leander answered defiantly.

"You fool," Ben answered, "I could spit
farther than we could see in that fog this
morning. We don't know where that damn
Injun went."

No, Dummy thought, he's a deer on
horseback. Dummy had seen him. He might
have corrected Pete had he made that
mistake, but he had learned better than to
advise Ben of anything.

"And if he's not behind us, then Whit
Whitman is," Bastrop added.

"We haven't seen Whitman since the

ambush," Leander countered. "We killed a deputy, maybe we scared him off."

Bastrop laughed. "You don't know Whit Whitman. He's about as single-minded as any man I've ever heard tell of."

Shrugging, Pete spoke to them both. "If anybody's behind us, they're gaining on us while we jaw this to death."

Leander and Ben turned to stare at Pete.

"As I see it," Pete continued, "some of us think this err . . ." He paused and twisted in his saddle toward Dummy.

Dummy smiled to let him know he was listening.

"Some of us think this deer on horseback," Pete said, as the others snickered, "is ahead of us and some behind us."

Dummy wasn't sure why all the men were laughing slightly, all but Pete. Didn't they believe him, that it was a deer on horseback?

"Maybe it's time to split up," Pete said. "Those that fear what's on our tail can continue, those that are scared of what's ahead can go back. Then whichever ones guess wrong will know it, if they live to tell about it."

Dummy considered Pete's proposal and figured it as wise as King Solomon's solution to the women claiming the same baby.

"Fine with me, Pete," Leander said, "but

only if Ben splits out my share of the loot."

"No doing," Bastrop answered instantly. "The money stays with me until I say it's time to split it up."

"Damn you, Ben," Leander shot back, his hand flinching nervously close to his revolver, "you've . . ."

"Ain't nothing you can spend it on out here, so what difference does it make, Leander," Bastrop answered, his eyes watching Leander's hand as if it were a snake about to strike.

"I'm entitled to my share. I earned it fair."

"Nobody says I'm fair, just boss," Bastrop replied.

"Ben," Pete broke in, "give him his cut."

"Yeah," Claude added. "Let him have it."

Bastrop's face puckered. "I'm outnumbered on this, Leander, but just don't expect us to save your worthless hide from either that Injun or Whit Whitman."

Leander nodded. "I'll take care of myself." He grinned. "My money."

As Bastrop dismounted to get Leander's share from the saddlebag, Leander maneuvered his horse between Pete and Claude, shaking hands with them. "Both of you are welcome to ride with me. Dummy, too, if you want to bring him, Pete."

"Nope," Pete said. "I feel better moving on."

Claude nodded his agreement, the bearclaw necklace around his neck clicking with the motion.

"Then boys, it's been a pleasure riding with most of you," Leander said, frowning as he turned back to Bastrop.

Bastrop shoved a fistful of bills at Leander. "Won't do you much good if Whit Whitman collects the reward on your head," he said. "What are you worth now, two hundred and fifty dollars? Just shows you're half the man I am."

Leander jerked the money from Bastrop's hand and took to counting. "The money's all I've been wanting, Ben. It better all be here!"

"Seventy-three hundred dollars was what we counted up after the take and we bought supplies in Mesilla. Dividing that by six gang members," Bastrop said, looking skyward as he figured, "and it came to twelve hundred and a few dollars. I was generous and gave you thirteen hundred dollars."

"Just a minute, Ben," Leander challenged. "I figure you owe me eighteen hundred and twenty-five dollars."

"What?" Ben yelled, lunging at Leander's horse.

The animal shied away and danced nervously until Leander settled him down. Leaning forward and patting his horse on the neck, Leander spoke. "Seventy-three hundred split up four ways is how I figure it. Prent's dead and Dummy don't count."

Dummy heard his name, but it wasn't true what Leander said. He did count, some. He could count to twenty and he could even add and subtract some, though multiplication and division were too hard to grapple with.

There was silence for a moment, everyone staring at Bastrop.

"Prent's dead and Dummy don't count," Leander repeated.

Dummy watched Pete nudge his horse between Ben and Leander. "You're right Prent's dead, but Dummy gets a full share."

"Now just a minute, Pete." Ben turned his watery eyes to Pete. "I promised Dummy ten dollars for keeping the horses for us. Nothing more."

"You figured him in the split until Leander called your bluff," Pete said calmly.

"Yeah, but as soon as we got rid of him, I was gonna split the remainder three ways. Been more in it for the rest of us," Bastrop answered.

"Except for Dummy," Pete answered. "Split it five ways, but Dummy gets Prent's share."

There was a hardness in Pete's voice that Dummy never remembered before.

Muttering, Bastrop kicked at a barren spot of ground, then picked up a twig and began to draw in the dirt. Funny time for Ben to be playing, Dummy thought until he realized Ben was doing some figuring with numbers.

"Seventy-three hundred split five ways," he said, scratching in the dirt with his stick, "comes to fourteen hundred and sixty dollars apiece." Ben stared up at Pete. "What's Dummy gonna do with that kind of money."

"Maybe it will buy him some help, a church home or someplace to take him in, look out for him, give him better company than we've made," Pete said, the softness returning to his voice.

Ben glanced up at Leander. "Split five ways, your take is fourteen sixty. You gonna bellyache about that?"

"Not if I get the rest of it now," Leander answered.

"By damn you can have it. But when you take it, your dealings with the gang is done." Grumbling as he retreated to his saddlebag,

Ben threw back the flap and pulled a railroad money bag out. Quickly, he counted out the remainder of Leander's split, then gave the bills to Pete. "Pass these to Leander. He'll want to count them."

Pete offered the money on to Leander who spent a minute thumbing through the bills, adding it all up.

"I'm satisfied," Leander said finally.

"Good," Ben answered. "It's time for the rest of us to get moving. Don't come running to us for any help."

Leander grinned at Pete and Claude. "I enjoyed knowing you. Claude, leave Ben at your first chance." Leander shook his head at Pete. "You do the same. I always found it hard to believe you was Ben's brother."

"Stepbrother," Pete corrected. "My pa married his ma."

"I always enjoyed your Bible reading, never said a thing though," Leander said. "Wished I could read."

"I had a good teacher. My pa was a preacher and he read it a lot. Everybody liked the way he read, everybody but Ben."

Leander smiled and nodded as if he had expected as much. "Bye, Dummy," he called.

Surprised, Dummy waved at Leander, wishing Pete were going with him so they could get away from Ben Bastrop. Dummy called out "Bye," at least that's what his brain meant to say, but his tongue got garbled and his ears didn't recognize the word. Ben Bastrop laughed, but no one else did and Leander rode away from them past Dummy and back down the trail, glancing occasionally back over his shoulder.

"Let's go," Ben Bastrop yelled, loud enough for Leander to hear.

Falling into line behind Bastrop and Claude, Dummy wanted to thank Pete for sticking up for him and his share of the money, but he wasn't sure what Pete had meant by a church home and he was confused about how much fourteen hundred dollars was. Was it fourteen or a hundred? Either way, it would buy plenty of licorice, which he'd share with Pete. Pete drew up beside him and offered Dummy his closed hand. Pete was always giving him things and taking care of him so Dummy stretched out his open palm and felt Pete press dried apple slices in his hand.

"Thanks, Pete," Dummy said, surprising himself. He always talked better when he wasn't nervous or trying to figure out how to put his feelings into words. He plopped a piece of apple in his mouth and shoved the others in his shirt pocket for later. The sweetness spread in his mouth until it seemed to coat his insides with a good feeling. The apple helped Dummy forget how tired he was. This riding all day, day after day, perplexed Dummy. Since Mesilla, they had avoided towns, avoided people and seemed headed nowhere in particular.

And Dummy still couldn't figure why the marshal would be after him. His ma and his brothers and sisters used to chase him when he was younger — before they turned ashamed of him — but they never hurt him. And now, so Ben said, this marshal was after them. Maybe it had something to do with the woman they had hurt. No, the marshal was chasing them before that. It must have been because of the train they'd stopped and the shooting. If the marshal caught up with them and threatened to spank him like his ma had when he was bad, Dummy wasn't sure he could explain that he had only held the horses. But the marshal might be mad because of the ambush and spank him anyway. He'd held the horses then, too, but wished he could have held his ears. The gunfire had exploded all around him and he had wanted to block out the noise, but he'd feared what Ben would do if the horses ran away. Dummy was just glad that his pistol didn't have bullets in it nor a trigger so it wouldn't make that terrible noise. Gunfire scared him, but the way the others had clung to the rocks during the battle made him think they were frightened as well.

And still, they rode to the west, as if they could catch the sun. But the sun had fallen behind that great peak they called White Mountain. Just a couple of more hours until a blanket of darkness would be drawn across the high country and it would be time to bed down. Dummy felt exhaustion hiding in every muscle and he needed sleep, but he wasn't so certain he could, not after what happened last night, not after the deer on horseback had slipped into camp and killed Prentice.

Up ahead, the country looked rougher, the valley they were following gradually narrowing into a chasm with deep, menacing walls. Dummy studied the terrain and didn't like it. It'd be hard to find a soft level place to pitch a bedroll. He reached a rock that reminded him of a locomotive and wished he knew where boulders that size came from. Maybe they sprang from the earth like plants. He leaned over the saddle to inspect the ground, but as he tipped away from his mount, he lost his balance for an instant. Struggling to right himself, he felt the dried apple slices fall from his pocket.

He wanted to stop for them, but Ben Bastrop might get angry or laugh at him, so he rode on.

But the others stopped ahead of him, all turning their horses to stare at him. How did they know? Then he heard it, in the distance, a popping noise. Dummy wasn't sure what it meant.

"Gunfire," Bastrop said, laughter accompanying his words. "Leander ran into the Injun or Whit Whitman. Dammit, there goes fourteen hundred dollars."

"You only care for yourself, don't you Ben?" Pete said. "I don't know why I stayed with you all these years."

Ben laughed, this time Dummy detecting a mocking tone like how his brothers and sisters once imitated his mistakes. "Sure you do, Pete. Your preacher pa with his last breath of life made you promise him you'd convert me from my sinning ways. Seems the joke's on the pious old fool. I've corrupted his son before he converted me." Ben laughed again.

Dummy felt sorry for Pete as he lowered his head. When Pete spoke, his voice was laced with shame. "I've wondered a thousand times why I made that promise, Ben."

"And I've asked myself as many times why you've kept it," Ben answered.

"I thought I could change you, Ben." Pete lifted his head and removed his hat.

"And your pa thought he could change my ma by marrying her," Ben said. "Seems you're like the rest of your kin, always making the wrong decision when it comes to the Bastrops. We're harder stock than your kind and don't believe in your heaven and hell."

"One day you will, Ben," Pete said, replacing his hat.

Then at once, Ben jerked his carbine from its saddle boot and Pete pulled his pistol. They turned their horses around toward Dummy who flinched at the sudden movement and feared for a moment Ben and Pete were going to shoot each other. Or him! Then Dummy heard the galloping hoofbeats behind him.

He thought first of the deer on horseback and twisted fearfully on his saddle, dropping his reins, his horse dancing nervously beneath him. It was Leander, slumped over his lathered mount, dashing toward them. Leander screamed something and Pete raced out to catch his horse. Leander's mount, its eyes wild with fright, veered away from Pete as he approached. Then Dummy saw the arrow shaft in Leander's chest and the red trail of blood on his shirt.

Pete caught the runaway's reins and eased the horse to a trot, then a walk and Leander slipped forward as if he might fall, but Pete managed to handle both him and the horse. Dummy watched in disbelief. Nobody had said anything, but he knew the deer on horseback had done this.

Galloping by to help Pete, Claude quickly reached Leander and to Dummy's disbelief, plucked him from the saddle as easily as he would a doll and held him baby-like.

"It was him," Leander shouted, the terror still in his voice. "Wearing those deer antlers and coming . . ." His voice trailed off into incoherence.

Behind him, Dummy heard Ben Bastrop growl. "Told you, you damn fool," he called as Claude carried him in and Pete led the horse back. "I told you not to come back," Ben said. "We're not taking you in, not now."

But Leander was hurt, Dummy thought, fearing Ben would leave him here for the deer on horseback until Pete spoke up.

"He's passed out, Ben," Pete called. "You're just wasting your breath."

"He's wasting our time," Bastrop replied. "Toss him, Claude."

Claude looked around at Pete, a look of uncertainty clouding his face, his shoulders drooping with doubt.

"Now just a minute, Ben," Pete said as he reached Bastrop.

"No, Pete, I told him we'd be better together, but he wanted to go it on his own. Couldn't abide by my decisions, couldn't trust me with his cut of the money."

"You don't turn away a sick man, that's not what the Good Book teaches," Pete answered.

"You and your Bible, always throwing it in my face. Well, dammit, you can take him in and care for him. I'll have nothing to do with it," Ben said, a smile suddenly exposing his rotten teeth, "unless . . ."

"Unless what, Ben?"

"Unless he pays up to rejoin us. I'd say fourteen hundred and sixty dollars."

Pete frowned. "Greed, Ben, that's all it is." Then he nodded. "If that's what it takes, you can have my share."

"Then he can stay." Bastrop stared west where the steep cliffs and boulders made a stand against the tall trees. "We won't make good time with him like that. We'll hole up in the canyon, wait for that damned Injun to come through, ambush him there and get him off our tail for good."

Ben turned to Claude. "We'll trap that damned Injun." Ben pointed to the huge rock beside the trail. "Take your carbine, canteen and bedroll and climb atop that rock. If the Injun comes this way, let him pass and we'll open fire when he reaches us. If we miss, you'll have a shot at him when he escapes. Think you can do that?"

Claude nodded. "What about Leander?"

"Drape him over his horse. Pete and I'll unload him up in the cover and we'll just wait for that Injun," Ben answered.

Dummy felt shivers running up his spine when Claude eased Leander belly down across the saddle. Claude was gentle, but still Leander groaned.

"Come morning, you can walk on in to camp," Bastrop said, "Dummy'll take care of your horses until then."

Claude said nothing more, just dismounted, gathered his gear and climbed atop the rock, vanishing behind it in a minute. Dummy hated to see Claude stay at the rock. It always felt safer to have a man Claude's size around, especially when a marshal and a deer on horseback were trailing you.

CHAPTER 10

The juices of the hunt boiling within him, Sulky yelled at the retreating White Eyes. The evil one had pulled his pistol and even managed four shots, before retreating pell-mell on his mount. But he would not ride long, not with the arrow embedded in his chest, not with the poison on the arrow tip.

This rider was a fool to ever leave the others, but he was a white man. They were all fools for they could not live off nature. Sulky shook the bow of strong mulberry wood at the retreating rider and winced at the pain which shot across his back. The grizzly hurt him yet, but the pain was only of the flesh. Deeper, in his bones, he felt the euphoria of a young boy on his first hunt, of a young man on his first raid. Had the White Eyes never come, then the Apache could still be warriors, could still be men.

But stopping the encroaching White Eyes was as futile as catching a cloud. Now the

Apache were trapped on reservations, as dependent on the Indian agent as a suckling baby at its mother's teat. No Apache was free any more, not since Geronimo had finally surrendered six years ago. For a moment, Sulky considered himself the last free Apache, but he knew that to be untrue. Bill Whitman was behind him and Bill Whitman would kill him even though, at one time, they had been friends. Even now, Sulky sometimes endured pangs of conscience for betraying Geronimo for the likes of Bill Whitman and the thousands of other White Eyes, thick as insects, who followed.

Taking up a palm-sized pouch, he tugged the leather strings shut on his cache of poison — festering animal blood, mixed with ground insects and harsh desert plants. The poison would not kill a man, but it would leave him too sick to be a man for several days, plenty of time for Sulky to find him and kill him.

Sulky opened the flap of his parfleche and slipped the poison pouch inside, his hand brushing the pitted metal of the revolver Geronimo had given him. Pulling the useless gun free, Sulky cocked the hammer and it groaned like his joints sometimes did on cold mornings. Once this revolver had belonged to a great warrior. And while in

Geronimo's favor, Sulky had received the pistol as a gift. Then he had betrayed Geronimo, had led the White Eyes soldiers to the great warrior's final hideout, had cast the fate of Apache men as little more than women. The rusty pistol hammer slipped from beneath his thumb and clicked sickly into place. Sulky no longer felt worthy of this gun.

If he was unworthy to hold the pistol, he carried another possession he no longer wanted. His free hand dug into his parfleche, his fingers wrapping around the dog-eared paper with a greasy sheen and jerking it out. The paper bore the signature of General George Crook, a letter which Sulky could not read. Red Beard had signed it for him before he was replaced by a lesser man, General Miles, who was less confident in Apache scouts than Crook. Geronimo, once found by Sulky, had surrendered to Crook one day, only to get drunk and escape the next to continue his warfare for six more months. Sulky hadn't been there for the final surrender because he had been mauled by the grizzly and he despised Miles. That was little consolation. Thumbing the pistol hammer, Sulky jammed the letter ahead of it, then released the hammer. It snapped, the paper impaled between it and the barrel.

Geronimo had given him a revolver. Red Beard had given him a letter. He was no longer worthy of the one, a traitor for ever accepting the other. In an earlier time, he had been considered a worthy successor to Geronimo. Now, he was unworthy to carry the broken gun of the great man. Sulky heaved a sigh and tossed the gun onto the trail the evil White Eyes had left.

Maybe after he killed those who had killed Dawn, he could take to the trail against other white men and murder them for Geronimo. Sulky removed the antlered headdress, then gathered his bow and arrows and parfleche and ran toward his hobbled horses, much as he had run as a youth when his father would wake him before sunrise, point out a distant landmark and command him to run there and back before taking a meal. It had built up his wind, his stamina, which even today was better than that of any white man he had ever encountered.

Sulky had always enjoyed running and had always obeyed when his father told him to run. His brother, though, had seldom complied and had usually run out of their father's sight and rested until time to return.

141

If they left together, then his brother waited for Sulky and raced ahead of him into camp, always humiliating Sulky before their father. His brother — Sulky never called his name because it was bad luck to speak the name of the dead — could never be trusted. His word changed like the wind and finally Sulky had had to kill him because of it. Sulky had given his word to a man and his brother had broken a trust upon which his own promise was built. His brother, and his uncle with him, had died because of that and if they had had two lives, Sulky would have killed them again for it. But it was bad to recall the deceased and Sulky tried to wipe the tracks of their memory from his mind.

It felt good to run and the horses tossed their heads and nickered at his approach, as if they enjoyed seeing him trot.

"I fast for man," Sulky called, "but never fast as horse."

After draping his load on the horses, he removed their hobbles and took their halters. He would run with them and give them rest. Leading them to the trail, he quickly picked up and followed the traces of the wounded White Eyes, occasional splotches of blood and the heavy fall of shod hooves on the soft ground. The hoofprints left singular impressions in the ground, not the double imprint when the back hoof fell almost directly atop the front hoof. With double impressions, the horse was walking or trotting, but this horse was running, the successive prints on each side about ten feet apart. The stride was wide and Sulky knew the horse, like the man, had been terrified.

When the valley curved gently toward White Mountain, Sulky stopped and mounted Ember. He pulled the deer head-dress from Ember's rump and lifted it atop his head, pushing it down securely in place. He patted the revolver and then the knife at his side.

Sulky knew this country and knew this valley around the bend funneled into a narrow chasm, strewn with rocks and hiding places for an ambush. Ultimately, the chasm would lead to another valley which marked the best route on horseback around White Mountain. Either the evil White Eyes knew this country or they were lucky in their trails.

Proceeding cautiously, Sulky guided his horses into the trees. The sun had dropped behind White Mountain, so the valley was enveloped in a shadow. And when the valley straightened toward the steep cliffs, Sulky halted and watched. Sulky stared for five minutes, studying everything from the huge rock the size of a cloud to the shadows deep within the chasm. He saw nothing, but then he heard nothing either, not even the sound of a bird, and that worried him.

Emerging from the deep shadows, Sulky picked up the wounded man's trail, following it until two other sets of tracks came out to meet it. Where the sets of tracks converged, the long strides of the terrified horse disappeared, and the prints of horses at a walk began. He alternately studied the tracks and the route through the canyon ahead. Nothing moved and nothing made a sound. He still spotted occasional drops of blood, but as he moved beside the great rock, his eyes saw a knot of ants swarming on the ground. He slid from Ember and landed softly upon the ground. Squatting over the ants, he slipped his knife from its sheath and brushed the swarming insects away. Then he jabbed the object of their frenzy and held it before his eyes. It was a dried apple slice and on the ground were two more. The evil White Eyes must be close, if the ants were still devouring that which they dropped. Sulky held the knife to his lips, blew off the final ant clinging to it, grabbed the slice between his teeth and pulled it from the knife, chewing it slowly.

He cleaned the two remaining slices, ate them and put his knife away.

Standing, Sulky noticed Ember's ears, then Bonita's, flinch forward. They had heard something. He strained his ears against the silence, but could make out no sound, not even a bird.

"Quiet, companions," he whispered to his horses, grabbing the halters of both, pulling them behind the rock and out of view from the canyon. Quickly, he hobbled both animals. He must climb the rock and study the canyon to see what was ahead.

"Quiet, my horses," he said, reaching for his Henry, then releasing it. He had but five cartridges for his carbine and it would hinder his climb because the rock, maybe twice his height, was steep here. He looked for craggy footholds up its sheer wall. Deciding on his route, Sulky grabbed at a crack in the rock and kicked his leg toward a foothold, his moccasins taking hold enough for his legs to boost him toward another handhold. His right hand, the one weakened from the encounter with the grizzly, slipped a moment and he thought he might fall until his nails dug into the ragged surface of the stone long enough for his legs to boost him to another handhold. He caught a quick breath, then froze, thinking for an instant that he had heard something. He wasn't sure what it was, but he knew it wasn't a bird. He shook his head and continued the climb, the antlers humping against the rock, the clicking seeming to echo across the valley. He heard another noise, maybe from above him, and then the whinny of his horses beneath him. He couldn't grab his revolver or knife without falling now.

His fumbling hands finally secured a hold atop the rock and he lifted his head. Over him, there was a sudden noise and by instinct, his head ducked at the blur aimed for his nose. Then he saw the boot. An instant later, he felt it glance off the side of his head, striking the antlers with its full force, the headdress flying off toward the ground.

Though stunned, Sulky knew he had but a fraction of a second to react. Or he would die! Above him a bear of a man loomed, still slightly off balance from the glancing kick. Sulky must strike quick like a snake. He lifted his head and with all the force his legs could muster, he pushed and then with his arms pulled his torso atop the rock.

But the big man swung his heavy boot toward Sulky. He dodged, but the boot slammed into his right shoulder, pain shooting like lava down his back. Gasping, Sulky grabbed for the attacker's lethal leg, catching it on the backward arc and shoving against it with all his might. The white man was strong and he hopped backward on his free leg, maintaining his balance a second longer until Sulky shoved again and his assailant stumbled over a breech in the rock. The big man crashed into the rock, his legs flailing against Sulky who held leech-like to his calf.

As his assailant gasped for breath, Sulky scrambled to his feet. His enemy was a big man and Sulky never remembered a bigger opponent, except the grizzly bear. Jerking his revolver from its holster, Sulky aimed it at his downed assailant. He tried to cock the hammer, but his arm was numb from his shoulder to his hand and he fumbled with the gun too long. His enemy was back on his feet, taking a menacing step toward him, his fists clenched like twin clubs. The big man drew back his fist to attack, but swung his foot instead at Sulky's gunhand. Sulky jumped away, but too late. Despite the numbness in his hand, he felt the pain as the heavy boot knocked the gun away. He dodged the big man's next lunge, listening for the clink of the pistol against the rock. But the answering sound was the nervous nickering of Ember and Bonita. His gun had fallen off the rock to the ground below.

"You'll die," the big man called, the words coming as a low growl from his throat, reminding Sulky of the great grizzly.

Sulky danced away from the big man, trying desperately to move from the edge toward the center of the huge rock, but the big man cut off his escape and he found himself too close to the edge. The slightest mistake and Sulky knew he would fall.

Standing still, the big man eyed him for an instant, then stamped his boot against the rock, like a bull before an attack. The moment's lull gave Sulky the chance to study his opponent. Standing half a foot or more over six feet, he wore a red flannel shirt over a blue checked shirt over his massive frame. The big man's eyes seemed to laugh with the confidence of a coyote moving in on a cornered rabbit and his slender smile seemed to confirm that confidence. His head, big and unscarred, was anchored to his huge shoulders by a tree trunk of a neck.

Then Sulky saw it.

The big man flung himself at Sulky, throwing his huge fists, but hitting only air where Sulky had been.

As he dodged the attack, Sulky caught glimpses of the big man's neck. His eyes had not deceived him. His assailant wore a necklace. A bearclaw necklace. His bearclaw necklace. The necklace Dawn had been wearing when she was murdered!

Distracted by the necklace, Sulky stumbled on the edge of the rock, teetering precariously an instant. The big man moved in and swung, missing with his right hand. Sulky felt the swoosh of the hand passing over his head, then the crash of the big man's other hand into his stomach. His mouth dropped open, sucking for wind, and his left hand fell to his stomach, then slipped to his side for the knife in its scabbard. He jerked the knife free of leather and lunged at his attacker.

The big man dodged the blade. "The knife won't save you," he growled.

Sulky stared at the necklace, his anger stoking his resolve to kill this man for what he had done to Dawn. He feinted with the knife, then sliced the air where the big man had jumped at the feint. His knife caught for a moment on the flannel shirt and ripped the fabric.

The knife snagged for an instant and the big man pummeled Sulky. Sulky saw the blinding approach of one fist, then saw a flash of light as it landed full force against his cheek. As he stumbled backward from the blow, he felt the other fist plow into his gut. The pain seemed to explode throughout his body and he wanted to scream, but he had no breath. He stepped forward, lunging blindly with the knife, taking a glancing blow off the side of his head. For a moment, he thought he was losing consciousness, then the sweet taste of blood in his mouth seemed to revive him, his senses groggy as if he were seeing and feeling everything through a fog. He felt the manacle grip of two overpowering hands on his wrist, the wrist with the knife. He pushed against the greater force, but it was like trying to move a mountain and all he could think about was the rattle of the bearclaw necklace and Dawn's death.

Then he heard the knife clatter on the rock at his feet. The sky was spinning around him and he feared he might collapse, his knees quivering with fatigue. When he blinked his eyes at his attacker, he saw not one, but two or more men and he could not tell which was real and which was not. Both man and mirage stepped back and Sulky knew his arms were free but numb. He shook them, but only a touch of feeling returned to his left.

His assailant laughed. "Now you'll die, Injun!"

Sulky saw the big man and his twin step at him. Sulky tried to swing one fist, then the other at him, but his arms only twitched. Sulky kicked at one of the approaching figures, but it was the mirage. Before his foot could fall back to the ground Sulky felt the iron grip of the other man tightening around his leg, then jerking him off his other foot. Sulky slammed against the rock, his head crashing against the edge, his brain swimming in pain.

Then a weight fell across his stomach and through his watering eyes, Sulky could see a dozen giant hands moving toward his neck and could smell the bile of his assailant's breath. He gasped for a deep breath as he felt two hands lock around his throat and tighten against his flesh. The pain came first in his throat, in excruciating spurts, then it sank down his chest into his lungs where his last breath was trapped and his whole body thrashed to expel it. Several times he seemed to totter between a fuzzy consciousness and an agonizing darkness. And every time he snapped out of the darkness, he was staring at the bearclaw necklace around the big man's neck. And his brain, screaming with pain, burst with memories of the great grizzly and of the nights he had slept with Dawn.

Sulky tried to lift his arms for the big man's neck and he thought his left hand had actually touched the bearclaw necklace. And when he knew he must do something or die, Sulky summoned all of his fading strength and bent his knees. Then with the explosive fury of a man seconds away from death, he heaved with his legs against the rock and shoved his body upward with so much force that the big man flew forward over Sulky's head, his iron grip pulling Sulky with him over the rim.

Sulky seemed to fly over the rock and linger in the sky until the big man, now hugging him around the shoulder, pulled him down from the clouds. They fell and fell and fell, as if there were no earth beneath them. It was a great exhilaration to fly and, most of all, to breathe again.

When his flight ended, it stopped with a tremendous jolt, the big man striking the earth beneath him, but cushioning his blow little. Sulky screamed in agony and felt the big man shudder once and melt away beneath him like a deer-gut water container suddenly pierced. Sulky drifted away, far away from this place. And out of the darkness, he saw the grizzly bear and he trembled. But shortly the grizzly disappeared like a vapor and in his hand he held the bearclaw necklace and someone took it from him and when he looked Dawn was wearing it and nothing else and he went to her and had her and nothing could be better than that. And then he fell into a deep darkness.

When he finally blinked his eyes open, he thought he was blind for he could see little. But it was night now. He shook his head, but the movement sent spasms of pain down his neck and into his shoulder. Slowly, his eyes began to focus and he could make out the moving forms of Ember and Bonita. He planted his hands on the big man's chest and pushed himself slowly up. It hurt to move, but the feeling had returned to his hands, the fingers on his left hand touching an unnatural hardness in the dead man's chest. His balance unsteady, Sulky wobbled for a moment as he straightened his knees and stood over his foe. He remembered the unnatural stiffness in the man's chest and the headdress that had gone flying over the rock.

Bending gingerly over the dead man, Sulky grabbed his shoulder and tugged. The body seemed rooted to the ground and Sulky struggled against his exhaustion and the weight of the dead man. Taking a deep breath which hurt all the way down his throat into his lungs, Sulky jerked the dead man over on his belly and felt the hide stuck to his back. It was as Sulky had figured. In the fall, his assailant had landed on the headdress, its antlers impaling his back. Planting his foot in the middle of the big man's back, Sulky grabbed the deer skull and worked it loose, stumbling backward when the bloodied antlers came free.

Slowly it came back to him that the others must be ahead and that Bill Whitman was behind him. But he must have rest from the beating. If he waited here, Bill Whitman might catch him. Though more evil White Eyes were ahead of him, maybe even waiting in ambush in the canyon, he preferred that risk to Bill Whitman. He remembered his pistol had fallen free and he had dropped his knife up on the rock, but he gave them up to the dark, reclaiming only the bearclaw necklace.

Sulky stumbled toward Ember, dragging the antlered headdress across the ground, then tossing it on Ember's back. He barely had the strength to loosen the hobbles on Ember and Bonita. Then as he tried to mount, Ember loomed over him like a mountain too high to climb. But by clawing at Ember's rawhide saddle and a handful of his mane, Sulky pulled himself atop the horse.

"Quiet, my horses. Let not evil White Eyes hear us," Sulky said as he shook the rawhide reins and Ember advanced toward the canyon, Bonita following. The horses moved quietly, reaching the mouth of the canyon, then moving deeper into it.

Some fifty yards into the canyon, Sulky felt Ember lift his head and whinny. Then from the side of the canyon, Sulky heard a couple of horses nickering. Ember stepped toward the noise and Sulky knew the horses were mares and Ember wanted to be with them. Sulky nudged Ember on. The evil White Eyes were near. And then Sulky heard a low moan and he nodded. It was a sick man's moan and Sulky knew his poisoned arrow was festering in the chest of another of the evil White Eyes. He would rest well knowing half the evil ones who had killed Dawn were dead or dying.

CHAPTER 11

Whit leaned forward in his saddle, then arose in his stirrups, staring at the trail up ahead.

Something was amiss, but Silas hadn't seen it yet. He was still wiping the sleep from his eyes, even though he had been in the saddle for better than an hour. Whit didn't linger when he awoke and that was always before dawn. How could he follow a trail before light? Maybe it was his damn intuition after all.

Whit settled back in his saddle and dug into his vest for more tobacco. No wonder he never ate breakfast, Silas thought. He always had his tobacco. Silas gnawed on a strip of jerky, but still his stomach felt as empty as the sky paling above him. The morning chill added to his discomfort and Silas wondered why he'd hired out as a deputy marshal. It was hard work, particularly with a man no more personable than a bear with a toothache.

Pulling back on the reins, Whit spoke for the first time this morning. "You see it?"

Silas studied the trail. He didn't want to make a fool of himself so early in the day.

"You awake, Silas?"

"I don't see nothing," Silas grumbled, mad at himself for showing his anger so early.

Whit pulled up his chestnut and dismounted, stooping over a patch of grass where his horse had dipped its head to graze. Poking his hand in the grass, Whit lifted a revolver, a piece of paper caught under its hammer. Thumbing back the hammer to free the paper, Whit pitched the pistol at Silas.

Unprepared, Silas dropped his reins, juggling the revolver from hand to hand until both palms trapped it between them.

"What Apache was the meanest, Silas?" Whit asked, unwadding the paper and staring at it.

Silas hated these blind questions, asked for no purpose but to humiliate him. "Geronimo?"

Whit nodded, still examining the paper. "You're holding a pistol that Geronimo himself used to kill many a white man."

Silas shook his head. "You expect me to

believe that? Geronimo's in prison."

"Hellfire and brimstone, Silas, don't you think I know that?"

Silas shrugged. "Anymore, I don't know what you know."

"This was Geronimo's revolver, while it worked. It was shot out of his hand during a fight with soldiers in Arizona. Never worked after that."

Silas doubted the whole damn story. "Did he throw it all the way to New Mexico Territory after the fight?"

Whit passed the paper to Silas. "You've seen this before. The gun, though, Geronimo gave it to Sulky."

Taking the paper, Silas held it close to his face to make out the writing in the dim morning light. It was the letter of introduction Sulky carried from General Crook.

"Before he turned Army scout, Sulky saved Geronimo in that fight. The old buzzard was surrounded, practically, and Sulky rode into the middle of that battle with a spare horse for the old chief."

It didn't make sense, Silas thought, handing the gun and letter to Whit. "Why'd he turn Army scout?"

Whit put the gun and letter in his saddlebag. "Who knows? Why would he throw this gun — a prized possession — away here?

Nobody knows an Indian's mind except an Indian and half the time even he's wrong about it."

"What makes you think he didn't just drop it?"

"Sulky does nothing by accident. Probably some foolish Apache custom or superstition. Who knows?" Whit climbed in the saddle and moved ahead.

They had ridden maybe twenty yards when Whit spoke again. "Looks like he got one." The marshal pointed at the ground.

Sure enough, there was a drop of blood between the hoofprints of a horse at a gallop. Silas nodded. "He caught up with them here."

"Hellfire and brimstone, Silas. Can't you read the damn tracks?"

Here it came again, another assault on his intelligence. Silas saw the tracks of several horses, heading to the west. It seemed as plain as the nose on his face or the scowl on Whit's.

"The gang's heading west, but one set of tracks came toward us at a walk until about there," he said, twisting in his saddle and pointing a dozen yards to the rear. "Now here are the tracks of several horses going west, all at a walk. One of them backtracked until Sulky caught him, but it don't make

159

sense why one came back."

Silas shrugged.

Whit noted where two sets of tracks converged. "Sulky took up after the rider here. Unshod horses." Whit scratched his chin. "If I could just make sense of it."

And if you could, Silas thought, the first thing you'd do would be to humiliate your deputy.

Whit said, "We'll know something soon. Sulky likes to finish his kills." His chestnut moved easily along as the marshal studied the tracks.

Silas watched, but nothing seemed to fit together, nothing that would confirm what Whit had already told him. Overhead, the sky had turned a pale blue and about them birds took up their calls, a particularly lonesome stellar jay following along behind them, serenading them with his shrill cry and pecking at their tracks for any insects that might have turned up.

The valley narrowed and turned to the south, then opened up toward a great rock beside the trail and a narrow canyon at the end.

"Hellfire and brimstone," Whit said. "Once Sulky gets them in that rough country, he can pick them off one at a time."

"Looks like he already got one," Silas said,

pointing to a body by the great rock beside the trail. "There goes more of your reward, Marshal," Silas said, smiling that Sulky might get them all, leaving Whit no reward money.

Offering no answer, Whit leaned over in his saddle and studied the hoofprints. Silas figured the marshal's silence was acknowledgement Whit had not seen the body. Silas aimed his horse to the near end of the great rock and the human heap at its foot. Behind him, Whit tarried, studying the trail. Drawing closer to the body, Silas realized it was that of a huge man.

It must be Claude Denham, Silas realized. Big though he was, Denham carried only a two hundred dollar reward on his head, his biggest vice mostly being that he had fallen in with the wrong company, like the kid that wasn't right in the head. Denham was sprawled on his stomach, a patch of dried blood spread across his back from two long, parallel gashes. Silas was puzzled by the wound.

Silas twisted in his saddle to check Whit, but he had disappeared. A simple panic touched his brain as he wheeled his bay around and blinked his eyes. He sighed when he saw Whit advancing along the trail, studying it closely, back now well beyond the big rock toward the mouth of the narrow canyon. Finally, Whit turned his chestnut around and headed toward Silas, taking his time to study the face of the big rock as he came. Then he evidently found what he was looking for because he kicked his horse into a trot.

"Thought you'd want to see the body before now," Silas offered.

Whit pulled up beside him. "He wasn't going anywhere."

Silas felt an anger welling in his throat. Whit and his damn condescension had left Silas with a bellyful of marshaling. On top of the rough trail life, Whit's company had made this as unbearable a ten-day stretch as he'd ever endured.

Whit dug into his vest pocket for his tobacco plug and whittled off a chunk, all the time studying the body. "Reckon you don't know him?" Whit said, then continued before Silas could answer. "Claude Denham, as big a man as ever broke the law."

The anger was simmering in Silas's throat. Anytime he knew something, Whit never gave him a chance to show it. Through his silence, Silas held his anger in check.

"Claude Denham," Whit continued, "a man so big, two hundred and sixty pounds, maybe, he always took an extra horse for when his first horse tired."

"Sulky finished him off when his mount tired?" Silas said.

"Hellfire and brimstone, Silas, Sulky never caught him."

"Dammit, Whit," Silas shot back, "we've trailed his blood for a mile or two. His horse was running, could easily have tired out with that load."

Whit folded up his knife and shoved it and his tobacco plug back in his vest pocket. Then he pulled open his vest and pointed at the tarnished badge. "That's why mine says 'marshal' and yours says 'deputy marshal.' I see things you're missing."

"I didn't miss the trail, nor the blood."

Nodding, Whit pointed toward the canyon. "You just turned away from it. The blood continues toward the canyon. A horse carrying as much weight as Claude Denham would've made deeper tracks than the ones we followed."

Silas swallowed hard. Whit had tied another kink in his line of reasoning and it was getting damn tiresome putting up with it. There were ways to tell a man he was wrong or wasn't as observant as he should be without insulting him to the bone. "Then how do you explain Denham's wound?"

Dismounting and handing Silas his reins,

Whit bent over and examined the body. "Never seen a wound like this before."

Silas felt a sly smile working its way toward the edges of his lips. He had the old fart now. He'd never figure it out.

Whit pulled a piece of blood-caked cloth away from the body, the cloth crackling as it tore free from the sticky flesh. Then, hunkering close to the body where Silas could not see what he was doing, Whit seemed to be plucking something from the cloth. Standing, he shoved his blood-stained fingers at Silas. He held something between thumb and forefinger. "You know what that is?"

Silas leaned over his saddle. "Sure, hair. Half dozen strands. So what if it's hair?"

The marshal frowned. "Anybody would know it's hair, but what kind of hair is it?"

Tiring of this game, Silas challenged him. "What difference does it make?"

"Plenty, if you want to figure out what killed him. And," Whit added, his words raising a challenge of their own, "if you really want to be a lawman."

Silas pulled the hairs from Whit's fingers and studied them. He couldn't tell much except they were tan or gray and short. Silas shifted uneasily in his saddle "Your gray wolf again?"

Whit took his reins from Silas. "Nope. Those are from the head of a mule deer." Whit climbed atop his chestnut.

"A deer damn sure didn't eat him. And if you are telling me a mule deer killed him, then this work is more dangerous than I figured," Silas replied.

"Silas, you got to open your eyes. You're looking, damn good about looking, but you're slow to see. What did Sulky take the night he slipped out on us?"

Here it came again, another line of inquiry bound to embarrass him. Damn Whit. Silas shrugged. "His weapons, his horses, his pouch." Nothing else came to mind.

"You're not seeing, Silas. He stacked a deer head with his weapons. It's a headdress the Apache use to stalk deer when they're hunting."

Silas couldn't hide the grin of disbelief working its way across his face. "You expect me to believe Sulky rode up behind Claude and gored him? I'm not that dumb, Whit."

"Just blind, Silas, not dumb," Whit began. "Best I can figure, the Bastrops have been splitting up to bushwhack Sulky. It was a damn mistake because no man with them is his match."

"That still doesn't explain how Sulky killed Denham with the horns, Marshal."

Whit nodded. "Denham climbed up on the big rock to ambush Sulky. The rock is marked near the front where he scratched his way up." Whit directed his horse past Silas's and between the rock and the body. He pointed to a pair of white scuffs trailing up segments of the rock. "Sulky climbed up the rock, expecting to surprise Denham, I'd guess. They had a fight and somehow Denham fell on the antlers."

It made sense, but Silas couldn't admit that to Whit.

Whit rode away from the rock and toward the trees. "Unshod tracks and horse droppings scattered out to here. He hobbled his horses before he climbed up and they wandered this far," Whit said then rode back toward Silas, stopping a dozen feet from the base of the rock and waving for Silas to join him.

Now what could it be, Silas thought, as he pointed his horse toward the marshal and rode over.

"All this happened after dark or Denham beat up Sulky awfully bad," Whit intoned, pointing to a scrub bush.

Silas spotted a revolver under the bush.

"Sulky wouldn't leave a usable gun unless he couldn't find it or didn't have the strength to look."

Silas saw his chance to shoot a hole in the marshal's guesswork. "How can you be sure the blood leading into the canyon isn't Sulky's?"

"The blood follows shod hoofprints past here. The blood continues before Sulky's trail joins theirs up the way."

Knowing he was whipped again, Silas rode out from behind the rock and stared toward the canyon. He didn't relish riding into that chasm. It reminded him of an open grave. Maybe it was that intuition that Whit always fell back on when he was stumped, but Silas knew better. He felt a shiver down his spine and told himself it was only the hunger pangs the jerky couldn't satisfy. But he knew better.

Whit said, "Let's ride."

It still bothered Silas not to bury a man, even if he had been an outlaw. "Just leave him for the varmints?"

Whit nodded. "We're getting closer to the Bastrops and I've figured out all I can from here. If we ride, we may catch them by dusk."

Silas shrugged, then scratched his chin. "There's one thing that's been puzzling me."

"Just one? Shoot," Whit replied.

"How do you figure all these things out?"

"For two years," Whit said, kneeing his chestnut and heading toward the canyon, "I scouted for the Army and learned from Sulky."

CHAPTER 12

The horses were restless and Dummy could hear them pawing at the ground and blowing at the sky. Peeking from under his blanket, he felt a kinship with them. The night had been long and terrifying. And what sleep Dummy had managed, had been interrupted by Leander at first moaning, then screaming at unseen demons. Pete had said Leander was delirious, but Pete hadn't explained what that meant.

Dummy heard a snort and clutched the blanket edge tight in his fingers. The noise had been close. His muscles tightened at the sound of another snort, like a wild pig grubbing for food. Dummy had never heard a deer noise before. Could this be the deer on horseback? His hand slid to his pistol. He must be brave. He must find out. He must warn Pete if it were.

As his hand inched the gun up beside his nose, he caught his breath and slowly rolled

169

over toward the noise. His hand trembled like a leaf in a slight breeze as he pulled the blanket edge down, over his forehead, to his eyebrows and then by his eyes. At the next sound, he shoved the pistol outside the blanket, pointing it at the bundle on the ground two paces away.

"Bang," he said quietly and then froze in terror.

He had shot Pete!

It was Pete who had been snoring, not the deer on horseback. A worse terror than he had ever tasted climbed from the knot in his stomach to his throat. He had shot Pete! His eyes misted and a tear rolled down his cheek. As he pushed himself up, he watched Pete's motionless form. Not a muscle moved. Dummy began to sob, softly at first, then uncontrollably. He lifted his hand to wipe the tears away and realized the gun was still in it. It frightened him and he tossed it away, not meaning to strike Pete's body, but the gun slammed into Pete's blanket.

Pete snorted, then shot up from his bedroll. Surprised, Dummy fell backward onto the ground, still crying, his hands balled at his eyes to dry their tears. When he brushed away his hand, he saw Pete squatted over him. Pete was safe after all!

"You okay, Dummy?" Pete's voice came as it always did, soft and reassuring.

Dummy shrugged. How could he explain to Pete what he had felt? He tried to speak, but only sounds, not words, came out.

"You scared, Dummy?" Pete asked, his hand reaching out and patting him on the shoulder.

Dummy nodded.

"It was a long night with Leander out of his head, but we made it okay," Pete said.

Dummy struggled to tame his tongue. "De . . . dee . . . deer?"

Pete glanced away from Dummy toward the big rock. "We're all scared, Dummy. Would you feel better if I read some?"

Dummy touched his lips and Pete retreated to his bedroll and found his Bible, thumbing through it as he returned. "If something happens to me, Dummy, I want you to have my Bible."

Maybe Pete feared he would shoot him again, Dummy thought, regretting the accident.

Seating himself by Dummy, Pete looked heavenward. "This is a passage about fear, called the Twenty-third Psalm. My pa favored it most among all the words of the Bible."

Dummy leaned against Pete's shoulder,

171

staring at the words on the page, making out one or two, but no more.

"The Lord is my shepherd; I shall not want," Pete started. "He maketh me to lie down in green pastures; he leadeth me beside the still waters."

They were pretty words, Dummy decided, but hard to figure because he was not in a green pasture, but on the hard canyon ground.

"He restoreth my soul; he leadeth me in the paths of righteousness for his name's sake. Yeah though I walk through the valley of the shadow of death . . ."

Dummy glanced around, wondering if this canyon were the valley of the shadow of death.

". . . I will fear no evil; for thou art with me; thy rod and thy staff they comfort me."

What were a rod and a staff? Dummy wished he knew more of these words.

"Thou preparest a table before me in the presence of mine enemies . . ."

That didn't make sense because they were running from their enemies, the two marshals and, worst of all, the deer on horseback.

"Thou anointest my head with oil; my cup runneth over. Surely goodness and mercy shall follow me . . ."

Just the two lawmen and the deer on horseback were following them, Dummy worried, and they were not goodness and mercy.

". . . all the days of my life; and I will dwell in the house of the Lord forever, amen."

Dummy watched Pete close the Bible and he had never looked so sad. Uncomfortable, Dummy tried to ignore the frown on Pete's pitted face, but it bothered him still, and he stared across the canyon to the spot where Ben had camped. With Ben on one side and Pete on the other, they had hoped to trap the deer on horseback, but he had not come. And somewhere out beyond the canyon mouth was Claude.

"I've done wrong, Dummy, letting you get involved in all this, thinking I could one day change Ben," Pete said, his voice cracking with the emotion. "Sometimes you're a better man by forgetting your promises."

Dummy wondered if Pete was suggesting that Ben would not give him the ten dollars for licorice as he had promised.

"You've the innocence of a child and you've seen things you'd no business seeing." His arm closed around Dummy and pulled him tight into his side.

Dummy didn't understand what Pete meant, but the hug reassured him that it would all work out one day. Pete's voice, though, was filled with a resignation much as he remembered in his mother's voice after he had grown as tall as her but not as smart as his little sister.

"A long time ago, I should have left Ben, never ridden with him. When we get Leander well enough to ride, we'll go our way and Ben can go his. Maybe we can leave this territory and find a place where we can become good folks, Dummy."

It would be good to abandon Ben Bastrop, to ride away from him, to escape his bullying ways, Dummy thought.

"I made a promise to my pa and shamed his memory trying to keep it," Pete said, his hand relaxing on Dummy's shoulder.

Dummy wanted to respond, but his mind seemed as muddy as a flooding stream and his tongue could never follow his thoughts so that they made sense to anybody but himself. He failed to fish out the muddled thoughts awash in his brain. He mumbled weakly, then managed two words. "Thanks, Pete."

Pete's hand softly patted Dummy's shoulder and told Dummy Pete had understood. At the sound of Ben's voice, Dummy felt Pete's hand harden on his shoulder.

"Pete, Pete," Bastrop called, his voice low

and ghostly. "Riders coming."

Pete's hand melted from Dummy's shoulder. "Damn," he said.

"Riders coming, Pete," Bastrop called again.

Was it the deer on horseback? He gulped at the knot in his throat and realized he was snapping his finger. He must get his pistol should the deer on horseback be near. He moved to stand, but Pete grabbed his arm.

"Stay low, Dummy, in case there's shooting," he warned.

Nodding, Dummy crawled over to fetch his pistol.

Like an evil wind, Bastrop's voice came again. "It's Whit Whitman, Pete. We've got to get him and his deputy this time."

Dummy, cradling the gun in one hand and absently dusting the dirt and grass from it, stared at Pete, motionless with his Bible open in his hands at his ears, his head bowed. He seemed to be reading it to himself. Dummy wasn't sure quite how one read to himself, yet no one nearby could hear it.

"Pete, you hear me?" Bastrop called, his voice louder now, taut with fear. "They're studying the big rock. Maybe they found Claude? Pete? Pete, wake up! We've gotta shoot them."

Pete stared up from his Bible, to the sky. "There's been enough killing, Ben."

"Don't turn righteous on me, Pete," Ben answered. "When the shooting starts, those bullets won't know the sinners from the righteous."

Pete didn't answer. He closed the Bible.

"You can have Leander's share, Pete, if you stick with me. What's it gonna be, Pete? They're getting closer."

Shutting the Bible, Pete called to Ben. "Pa always said the right decision is the hardest to make because the devil has you believe there's an easier way, like killing the marshal."

"Dammit," Ben called, "quit preaching!"

Dummy crawled back to Pete, thinking he would roll up his blanket, but Pete just sat there, staring into the sky. Dummy watched Pete's lips mouthing words and he recognized them as the same words Pete read moments earlier. Strange, Dummy thought, that Pete could read the words again without opening the Bible.

"They're getting closer, Pete," Ben called. "Between the two of us there's a lot of money we could divide up."

Pete spoke to himself. "Greed's ruined us."

"Last chance, Pete. You know I've got all

176

the money in my saddlebag here. You'll share in it," Ben called back.

Pete crouched and moved to a vantage point overlooking the trail twenty feet below. Dummy crawled behind him, then peeked between two rocks toward the sun. He made out the silhouettes of two riders halfway between the canyon mouth and the great rock where they had last seen Claude.

"Keep low, Dummy. This is Ben's fight. He's had an evil pull over us too long," Pete whispered. "Our responsibility is to ourselves from now on."

Dummy nodded, knowing his responsibility, as always, was the horses. They were staked and hobbled below, but out of sight from the trail. If he crawled back past his bedroll, he could look down upon them. With Prent dead, Leander dying and Claude missing, Dummy had four additional horses, plus his own to saddle up. Dummy worried how he could explain to the marshal that he had only held the horses.

Glancing across the narrow stretch of canyon, Dummy spotted Ben scrambling among the rocks for position and carrying his carbine, his canteen and his saddlebags with the train money.

"Get down, Dummy," Pete ordered. "The riders are nearing." Pete ducked behind the boulder and squatted into it.

Dummy felt his heart pounding in his chest, keeping a steady beat with his snapping finger. There would be shooting and it would be loud and frightening. Dummy thought of his blanket and considered crawling under it, pulling it over his head, but Pete might laugh at him. Dummy saw Pete close his eyes as if he were hiding from something himself. Shortly, Dummy heard the muffled hoofbeats of the approaching riders. Otherwise, the silence was frightening and almost unending.

And then it came, to Dummy's relief because the wait was over, the first shot, not once, but twice as it echoed down the canyon. Dummy flinched, but Pete never opened his eyes.

Beneath him Dummy heard two men shouting at their spooked horses as they took cover. Another shot crashed through the canyon and Dummy shielded his ears with his hands. The noise came like thunder, the lead of the unseen lightning ricocheting down the canyon. Dummy could hear one of the lawmen yelling. Still, Pete, his eyes still closed, hadn't moved.

From just down the canyon, Dummy heard the galloping hoofbeats of a horse on the loose. The animal ran deeper into the canyon, causing a stir among the horses that were his charge. Through his hands, at his ears, he heard the lawmen peppering Ben's hideout with bullets.

"Get 'em, Pete," Ben screamed. "You can get 'em from behind." The lawmen answered his plea with gunfire.

The retorts of the guns echoed down the canyon, each shot seeming louder to Dummy than its predecessor.

"Give up, Bastrop," came a strange voice Dummy had never heard before. It was a hard voice, but in some ways less threatening than Ben Bastrop's, Dummy figured. "We found Claude by the big rock. He's dead. You better give up before that Apache gets you like the others."

What Apache? Dummy couldn't figure it out. All he knew trailing them, besides the lawmen, was a deer on horseback.

"Beats the hangman," Ben cried out, sending another volley into the rocks below.

"You got a chance with a jury, but none with the Apache," the hard voice called back.

They traded shots, pausing only to reload, but in the intermittent quiet, Dummy heard the sounds of movement below him.

After a flurry of shots, Ben screamed across the canyon. "Dummy, the horses!

Take care of the horses like I ordered you. They're moving for the horses."

He had forgotten! Pete might be mad, too, Dummy thought. He shot up from the ground, seeing Pete's eyes flutter open as he did. Pete must not know he had forgotten his chore. Dummy dashed for the path leading down to the horses. He tripped over his bedroll and almost fell but managed his balance somehow.

"No," he heard Pete yell behind him. Then he caught the sound of the rocks around him thudding, each thud followed by the crack of a gun. "No, Dummy, get down!"

Dummy's heart jumped to his throat. Get down, Pete had said. He must get down to the horses and saddle them so they could escape. Reaching the path, he placed his hand on a rock and turned a final time to look at Pete. Pete was up on his feet and charging after him.

As he turned toward the horses, he heard another thud into the rock. He felt an instant stinging in his face, sharp pains stabbing at his cheeks. He fell to the ground, his hands grasping at his face.

"No, dammit, no," Pete shouted. Then Dummy heard the sound of gunfire close by and realized Pete was firing back.

Dummy lifted his hands from his face and

cried at a trail of blood smudged on his palm. He wished for his mother, but Pete was beside him in an instant, his gun still smoking.

Pete brushed Dummy's hands away and ran his fingers down Dummy's cheek, stopping at the most painful point and pressing against the cheekbone. "You're okay, Dummy. Just a chip of rock stung you."

Too scared to try to say anything, Dummy nodded.

"We'll work our way down to the horses and ride out of here," Pete said, breaking open his pistol and dumping the hulls at his feet. He pulled cartridges from his belt and shoved them into the pistol chamber.

Dummy sat up. He could feel a trickle of blood trailing down his cheek, but Pete had said he would be okay.

Pete darted to a rock and started shooting. Dummy crawled to Pete to help, pulled the broken revolver from his belt and peeked down below. Seeing a man, Dummy aimed and squeezed the trigger guard. "Bang," he yelled as loud as he could. Shouting "bang" just as Pete's gun exploded beside his ear, Dummy saw the man he'd aimed at drop his gun and grab his arm.

"Get away, Dummy, to the horses," Pete screamed.

Dummy was glad to obey for Pete's last pistol shot was still ringing in his ears.

"Saddle up three, quick," Pete commanded. "Get our canteens and take the extras. Forget the other horses. And take this."

Dummy nodded, accepting Pete's Bible and stuffing it and his pistol in his pants, then stumbled to his feet, circled the bedrolls, grabbing his and Pete's canteens, and scrambled down the path to the horses. He slipped once and landed hard on his tailbone, jarring his teeth. Pushing himself up, he scooted down the rocks, like a crippled goat. Reaching the horses, he found them as nervous as himself, tossing their heads, stamping their feet, nickering at the gunshots resounding through the canyon.

Pete called from above. "Hurry, Dummy."

Dropping the canteens, Dummy jumped toward his own saddle, grabbing the saddle blanket and running with it to his gray, the mare flinching as he tossed the blanket over her and smoothed it down across her back. He stepped back for his saddle, took a deep breath, picked it up and heaved it across the animal's back, working fast to cinch it up.

"Faster, Dummy," Pete implored.

Dummy scrambled among the saddles for Pete's. It seemed to take him forever, before he recognized the well worn saddle and its scarlet saddle blanket. Grabbing them both, Dummy stumbled toward Pete's dun, the horse fighting its hobbles. He wanted to say something to the horse, to calm him, but his own tongue was paralyzed with fear. Quickly, he fitted blanket and saddle to the horse's back and his fingers fumbled to tighten the cinches.

Now he would saddle Ben's black, which was bucking against its hobbles, finally jerking its stake rope free. Grabbing Ben's saddle blanket, Dummy ran at the black, but it backed away on its hobbles. Dummy slowed and approached the animal at a walk, but as he neared and threw the blanket at its back, the black jumped at the sound of gunfire and the blanket fell to the ground.

"Let's make a run for it, Pete," he heard Ben shout.

Not much time, Dummy knew. He started for the saddle blanket but the black trampled over it and Dummy gave up, retreating for Ben's saddle, hoisting it with his two aching arms and advancing toward the black which shied away from each step until it was backed up against the canyon wall. Dummy took aim with the saddle, then lunged toward the horse, the saddle falling in place on the black's back. His hands

183

worked better now but the black compli-
cated the cinching by bucking against its
hobbles. Finally, the saddle was tight and
Dummy heaved a sigh.

Then Dummy heard a commotion on the
path. It was Pete, stumbling among the
rocks. "Good boy, Dummy," Pete called.
"Unhobble yours, mount and get ready to
ride."

Dummy started to do that, then remembered he'd forgotten all the canteens. He
dashed among the saddles, exasperating
Pete until he realized what Dummy was collecting. As he picked up the mostly empty
canteens, they clattered one against the
other as he retreated to his horse and
mounted.

"Hang onto the canteens," Pete commanded. "We'll need them."

In the saddle, Dummy draped the straps
of all the canteens over his neck. Pete ran
beside Dummy's mare, stooping for an
instant, then tossing the hobble strap across
Dummy's saddle.

"When we hit the trail, gallop your horse
away as fast as you can. I'll take Ben a horse
and we'll be right behind you." Pete untied
the gray's stake rope and tossed Dummy
the reins.

Pete untied his horse and unhobbled

184

Ben's black which bolted for freedom, but Pete had wrapped the reins around his hand and tugged sharply against the animal, bringing it under control long enough for him to mount his own horse. Pete yelled, "Ride, Dummy, ride."

Dummy slapped the flank of his mare and she darted onto the trail, the canteens bouncing against himself and each other.

Behind him, he heard a flurry of gunshots. Shortly, he heard little but the sound of his horse's hoofbeats and the canteens beating against one another. He looked back over his shoulder to see if Pete and Ben were following, but a cold shiver raced up his back. He saw neither, but on a high rock near the trail, he thought he saw a deer standing on its hind legs, silhouetted against the early morning sun. Dummy closed his eyes and let his mare run as she pleased through the canyon.

CHAPTER 13

"Get him, Silas," Whit screamed, his words tinged with pain.

Thumbing cartridges into his Winchester .44 carbine, Silas heard hoofbeats and bolted from his den onto the trail, glimpsing the back of one rider making it around the bend, then a second galloping toward him, a spare horse in tow. Levering a bullet into the chamber, Silas aimed at the horseman's back.

"Shoot him, dammit," Whit yelled again.

His finger tightening against the trigger, Silas felt the carbine's recoil in his shoulder and smelled the acrid powder. He cursed the rider for swerving to the canyon wall and the bullet for missing.

A second man scrambled from the rocks, carrying a set of saddlebags, a canteen and his rifle. Silas dropped down to a knee and propped his carbine on a rock to steady his aim.

"That's Ben Bastrop, Silas," Whit kept yelling. "Get him."

Just as Silas squeezed the trigger, Bastrop spun around, lifting his rifle half way to his shoulder and firing. At Silas!

As Silas jumped to the ground, the bullet pinged into the rock behind him, sparks flying in its wake. Too close!

"Hellfire and brimstone," Whit bellowed. "Get him."

Dammit, the old fart could do some shooting himself. He still had one good arm. Lifting his head to find Bastrop, Silas heard a whine, then the shot, and felt his hat yanked from his head. The hot breath of lead scorched his hair. Dammit! He ducked, running his fingers over his scalp. Expecting blood, he flinched at the wetness in his hair. But lowering his hand and wriggling his fingers before his eyes, he sighed. They were sticky — with sweat.

Hearing hoofbeats, Silas rolled to another boulder and came up in a crouch, his carbine pointed down the trail.

Whit was yelling, "You're letting them get away."

Silas fired, levered out the empty and fired again and again until the pull of his finger brought only the click of empty.

"Hellfire and brimstone," Whit was shouting. "If they'd winged you instead of me, I'd a had them."

Silas gritted his teeth. Fact was, they did get him and for the second time in a week Whit had led them into an ambush. "Where's your intuition, Whit? You should've felt the bullet coming and moved."

"Deputy," Whit answered, "they shot my horse from under me. The fall knocked the breath and intuition out of me."

Silas knew what he'd like to knock out of Whit because he was as full of it as a towsack of manure. "You need tending?"

"Check my horse first," Whit replied.

Silas nodded, and for the first time since the shooting started, wondered about his bay's whereabouts. Silas saw the chestnut, sprawled across the trail and knew it was dead. Whit would have the excuse that his horse was killed, but Silas couldn't avoid the blame for his loss. All he remembered was jumping out of the saddle, grabbing his carbine from the boot and heading for cover at the first shots, all evidently aimed at Whit. Silas squatted over the chestnut. "He's dead!"

Whit answered, "There's a bottle of whiskey in my saddlebag. If it didn't shatter in the fall, bring it to me."

"Yeah," Silas replied. Silas would've bet his share of the reward money — if he were even getting a share — that Whit wouldn't offer him a single sip.

"And the canteen," Whit called back.

Moving to the horse's rump and still holding his carbine, Silas unbuckled the strap on the left bag and stuck his hand inside, brushing aside a fresh shirt and box of cartridges, but retrieving a metal frame. He examined the gold tinted frame and the fading tintype it encased. A woman with long ringlets of hair seeping out of her bonnet held a girl no more than two years old in her lap. On her shoulder rested the hand of a young man, a stiff smile on his face. Silas was shocked. He had never before seen a smile on Whit's face. Whit was younger then with black hair, but the same set of the jaw and the determination of the eyes endured even until today.

"You taking a nap, deputy," Whit called.

Silas shoved the tintype back in the saddlebag and reached to the bottom, his hand closing around the stubby neck of a liquor bottle. Extracting it, Silas saw the bottle was full. Damn if Whit didn't have discipline, he admitted. Better than a week on the trail and the bottle was unkissed by thirsty lips. "I found it," he called.

189

"About time," the marshal answered.

Silas rose slowly and walked even slower to Whit's hiding place, tempted all the way to smash the bottle on the rocks.

Finding Whit, Silas propped his Winchester against a rock and kneeled down beside him, squeamish at the marshal's blood-soaked sleeve. Maybe this was more serious than he had first thought. "You gonna make it?"

"What difference does it make?" Whit said, releasing his right hand from his left arm.

"Whether or not I have to dig another grave," Silas said, deciding the loss of blood hadn't improved Whit's disposition.

The marshal flinched as Silas touched his shirt sleeve wet with red. Unbuttoning the sleeve, Silas pulled it up over the wound about midway between his elbow and shoulder. Great beads of sweat rolled down the marshal's face.

"It pains me, but I can still move my arm. I figure it's just a flesh wound," Whit said matter of factly, as if he were talking about someone else.

"Ready for a drink?" Silas asked, working the stiff cork loose from the bottle.

"Pour some in the wound," Whit commanded.

190

"A waste of whiskey." Silas smiled, but Whit only scowled.

"Do as I say," Whit answered. "It may save my arm."

Silas grabbed Whit's arm tight and tipped the lip of the bottle toward the oozing wound. Silas felt the marshal's arm flinch, then stiffen as the amber liquid dripped into the wound. Lifting the bottle neck, Silas worried about Whit's paleness. "You okay?"

Whit nodded. "You got a clean bandanna on you?"

"Nope, what you . . ."

"In my saddlebag, I've a clean shirt for a bandage."

Silas corked the bottle and retreated to the chestnut. Squatting over the dead animal, he reached into the saddlebag, pulling out the shirt and the tintype tangled within its folds. He started to untangle it, decided against that, and carried the wadded shirt and frame back to Whit. The marshal's eyes were closed, but gradually they opened at Silas's noise.

Silas handed Whit the shirt and the marshal's hand dropped quickly from the extra weight of the framed tintype. Working with his good hand, Whit quickly dug the tintype from the folds of the shirt and laid the frame face down against his chest.

"I saw it when I got the bottle, Whit," Silas admitted. "Nice looking family."

Whit ignored him. "Tear off a sleeve."

Taking the wadded shirt from Whit's stomach, Silas held it against his chest, a hand clasped on each side of the shoulder seam and pulled against the threads. They held for a moment, then ripped apart.

"Soak the sleeve with whiskey," Whit commanded, "then give me the rest of the shirt."

Silas obeyed.

"Now, cover your little finger with the cloth and poke it through the wound."

"What?"

"You heard me. Once you get your finger through, leave the cloth inside and pull your finger out. Grab the cloth at both ends and pull it back and forth in the wound. Then pour more whiskey on the wound." Whit held the rest of the shirt to his mouth. "This'll keep me from screaming, but if I pass out, pull it from my mouth so I won't strangle, then use it to bandage my arm." Whit stuffed the shirt in his mouth.

Silas felt a queasiness in his stomach, but he wrapped his little finger in the cloth, then grabbed Whit's arm and eased his finger over the wound. Silas took a slow, deep breath, then jammed his finger into the wound.

Whit jerked against the pain, his feet thrashing for a moment, muffled moans describing the agony.

Sliding his other hand up Whit's quivering arm to the exit point of the bullet, Silas felt his little finger protruding from it. Quickly, he pinched the point of the cloth between his fingers and jerked his little finger clear of the wound.

Whit gasped.

After grabbing both ends of the cloth, Silas worked the cloth back and forth through the wound as if he were cleaning the barrel to his pistol. Then, releasing one end, he grabbed the liquor bottle, uncorked it with his teeth and soaked the cloth and the wound with whiskey.

Whit stiffened with pain, his arm jerking up against the bottle, almost knocking it from Silas's hand, then falling to the ground, limp. He had passed out, the framed tintype sliding from his chest to the ground.

Silas poured about a third of the bottle on the wound, corked the bottle, then tugged free the shirt Whit had clenched between his teeth. The marshal's breath was unsteady.

"Well, you old fart, looks like you'll be out

193

for a while," Silas said. "Guess I'm in charge now."

Whit moaned once, then his breath grew more regular.

Silas finally pulled the cloth from the wound, then doused it with more liquor and wrapped it tight around his arm, covering it with the rest of the shirt. "That'll have to do, Marshal." Silas took off Whit's hat, then shoved it between the marshal's head and the rock he was propped against. The tintype, which had slipped to the ground, he slipped under Whit's hand.

Now, Silas thought, he'd find his own hat and, if he were lucky, his own horse. He didn't relish Whit waking and learning they were horseless. What he needed was a good drink, so Silas unplugged the bottle and downed a healthy swig, then another. It went down with a kick. It wasn't good whiskey, but Whit most likely bought it for medicine anyway. Silas corked the bottle, then picked up his carbine and reloaded it in case the Bastrops came back or, even worse, Sulky showed up.

With carbine in hand, he climbed back over the rocks, looking for his hat. In ten minutes, he had found it as well as counted thirty-three empty hulls from his carbine, a lot of bullets spent for no more results than he'd gotten. Picking up his hat and dusting it off, he studied the crown and shook his head. He shoved his little finger in one hole and out its mate and watched it wriggle. He shrugged, pulling his finger from the damaged felt, and fitted the hat tight around his ears.

Now he must look for his horse. From up the canyon, he heard Whit groan, the canyon walls distorting the sound until it seemed to come from the opposite side. Whit would have to make it on his own for a while, Silas thought, as he clambered up the rocks, starting little rockslides as he moved ever higher for a good vantage point to take in the canyon and maybe his horse. Above him the sun was still climbing but it wouldn't be long until noon. Hunger still gnawed at his stomach and he longed for a good hot meal, back in civilization. Climbing about as high as he cared to, Silas crawled out onto a solid rock shelf, lay on his belly and studied the canyon as far as he could see. Behind him the entrance was steep and narrow, though it widened some ahead. Beyond that it disappeared behind a bend. The canyon rim was studded with pines and other trees, but mostly stunted trees dotted the walls wherever soil cropped out between the rocks.

He spotted beneath him a level patch of

high ground where two bedrolls had been left. Just below the bedrolls he took in something that made his heart flutter. Horses. They were screened by some scrub brush and Silas had to wipe his eyes a couple of times to be sure he wasn't imagining things. He wasn't.

Silas clapped his hands and looked down at his badge to wipe a smudge from it, figuring if he wasn't a good deputy at least he was a lucky one. Silas hopped off the big rock, stumbling as he hit the ragged incline, his boot heel jarring loose a small slide of rocks that dripped down the canyon and finally stopped twenty feet away at the base of another boulder. He moved more carefully to avoid creating a bad slide.

Finally, he reached the natural rock corral. His bay stood with four other horses, all but his staked and hobbled. Four saddles were scattered on the ground. He heard Whit groan again and a fear crawled up his back like a centipede. This canyon was making him goosey. Whit was back down the canyon, but his groans seemed to carry from across the way, then echo off the canyon walls into oblivion. Then it struck Silas and he counted the staked horses, four plus his own stood before him.

Another moan meandered eerily down the canyon.

Silas started counting. Two outlaws were dead and one of them always rode with an extra horse. That explained three of the horses below, but Silas recalled seeing only three outlaws ride away. One was the kid touched in the head, another was Ben Bastrop and the third he didn't know. Six had started out with the outlaws but that only accounted for five.

Another moan came.

Silas whistled to himself, then lifted his carbine and checked the load. That wasn't Whit moaning. One of the Bastrops had been left behind. Was it a trap? Silas realized he had never felt more alone in all his life. He took a deep breath, sliding his finger over the trigger. He hid for a moment between two rocks, studying the rock wall opposite him. At the next moan, he dashed across the canyon and worked his way among the rocky cover. For an hour, he chased the elusive groans. He never realized sound could be so deceptive. And when he finally spotted the wounded man, Silas was thirty yards down canyon and above the man, who languished in a level patch among the rocks. The outlaw twitched occasionally in the brightness of high sun.

Silas angled back down the rocky slope, cursing softly at the rocks and dirt which gave way beneath his boots and cascaded before him like a gritty carpet being rolled down his path until he reached his quarry. The outlaw had a soft face with a trace of blond whiskers lying like thread stubs around his parched lips. His blond hair was matted from sweat and his shirtless chest heaved with each irregular breath. Most of all, Silas noticed his putrid shoulder, discolored with purple and green splotches of flesh, a nasty wound as dirty as death. Flies waded in its seepage around the broken shaft of an arrow.

Silas swept the flies away with a brush of his carbine, then placed it by the wounded man and picked up the canteen at his side. "Water?" he said, shaking the canteen. Unplugging the canteen, he dripped some over his fingers and brushed them against the outlaw's burning lips which slowly parted for his swollen tongue to lick them, then his eyelids squinted open against the brilliant sunlight.

"Water?" Silas repeated.

A slow, deliberate nod seemed to rob the man of his last ounce of strength. Then he struggled to lift his head, but failed. Tilting the canteen with his right hand, Silas slid his left between the blanket and the man's neck, then lifted.

"Yeaoooooww," the outlaw screamed, jerking free of Silas's grasp and slamming back into the ground. "Ahhhghhh," he cried.

Instantly, Silas dumped water into his palm, letting it trickle into his open mouth. He gave water that way until the canteen was dry. Damn if Sulky wasn't going to get them every one, provided Whit didn't catch up with him first and Whit seemed as anxious to corner Sulky as any of the outlaws. Silas looked at the one sprawled before him and knew this one wouldn't live long enough for anyone to take back. There wasn't much he could do, Silas figured, so he best get back to Whit and check on him.

Taking his carbine, Silas noticed twenty or more spent cartridges scattered around. This had been Ben Bastrop's vantage point when the shooting started. Silas looked down over the trail and admitted he was probably lucky to be alive. The view was perfect for a kill. A man had only so much luck in his pocket and Silas wondered if he was running as short of it as he was of patience with Whit. But damn if he wanted Whit to die, not now, at least, because Silas knew he'd have to dig the hole to bury him and Whit wasn't worth the effort.

Easing back down the slope, Silas flushed a rabbit from a bush and his mouth watered from the thought of meat to fill his sulking stomach. The rabbit stopped about a dozen yards down the trail and Silas lifted his carbine, aiming for the head. A hit at such close range would tear up too much of the meat if he aimed for the body. He squeezed the trigger and the rabbit flipped in the air from a perfect shot. Silas scooted along the rocks to the rabbit and grabbed its hind legs, then toted it to the rock where Whit lay.

When Silas stepped around the rock and spotted Whit, his heart climbed into his throat and the rabbit tumbled from his fingers. Whit was sitting there with his eyes open and his revolver in his hand, pointed right at Silas's heart.

"The shooting, Silas, what was it about?"

"A rabbit, I killed us a rabbit for some meat."

Whit, his face pale, shrugged. "Feared it was Sulky coming back to get me."

Whit seemed calm, but was the loss of blood affecting his memory? "You mean the Bastrops? Coming back after us?"

"Hellfire and brimstone, deputy, I mean Sulky. And I mean him coming back after me, not you."

It was beyond Silas, he turned to scavenge for enough wood and brush for a fire, wondering if Whit were delirious. After he gathered an armload, he returned to Whit, built a fire, cleaned the rabbit, then roasted it quickly, the flames crackling and spitting sparks at the greasy meat as Whit watched.

"One of the Bastrops is wounded, denned up across the canyon. Doubt he'll last until morning," Silas offered.

Whit said, "It must be the one Sulky got."

Silas nodded his head, not quite certain how Whit had figured it out. "How'd you know? Silas asked, twisting the purple rabbit meat slowly over the fire as it crusted brown from the flames.

"Knew I didn't wing one of them and figured you didn't either."

Silas bit his tongue and swallowed the salty taste in his mouth. If he could make a meal of Whit's insults, Silas knew he'd be a fat man forever. He stood over the fire, its flames dying away like his desire to be a deputy. Figuring the rabbit as done as it would ever be, he jerked it from the stick and ripped it in half, the hot sting of the meat in his palm not nearly as biting as the sting of Whit's words. He handed the marshal his half.

Grabbing the meat, Whit dropped it on

his shirt. "Ouch," he said, "it's hot enough."

Silas gobbled his own down silently. Tossing the bones aside, Silas wiped his hands on his britches and studied the badge on his chest. It was just tin, nothing more. Like the job, it promised more than it could ever deliver. No wonder the marshal never put a shine to his tarnished badge.

"I've the horses to attend and the wounded man across the way to give a drink, if he's still alive," Silas said.

Whit nodded. "You know which one it is?"

Silas shrugged. "I don't know the bad men like you do."

"Just wondering how much reward money we lost," Whit said, around a bite of rabbit meat.

"We?" Silas spit out. "Last I heard, I got paid monthly wages and you got all the reward money."

"With me wounded and Sulky still on their tail," the marshal said, "it's doubtful we'll get a reward anyway."

Silas spun around on his heels and stomped toward the horses. He spent the afternoon finding them grass to eat and a spring for water, stripping Whit's dead chestnut of its saddle, toting fresh canteens of water to the outlaw, going through the gang's abandoned gear and checking Whit occasionally.

Eventually, the day's shadows melded together and Silas plodded exhausted into camp, Whit greeting him with his snores. Silas moved quickly to lay out his bedroll and claim some sleep of his own. He fell upon his blanket and it was as if he had dropped into some deep dark well, sleep drowning out his exhaustion.

The next thing Silas recognized was the sound of Whit's voice, as if it were coming from outside that well. Gradually, the voice sounded near, not distant. "Time to get up," Whit was saying.

Knowing he had just gotten to sleep, Silas felt anger racing with the blood through his veins. But cracking his eyelids enough to look out at the world, he realized it was daylight. He turned over and rubbed his eyes, then looked up at Whit. The marshal stood over him, his hands on his hips, looking drained from the wound.

"It's mid-morning, but I figured you deserved the rest for all the work you've done," Whit said. "Show me the one they left behind — I haven't heard him all morning — and then we'll ride."

In a matter of minutes, Silas was working his way up the opposite side of the canyon, Whit following him, but not with his usual vigor. The wound had sapped his energy. Topping a final rise in the rocks, Silas pointed to the wounded man. "He's still alive," he said in disbelief.

Whit caught up with Silas shortly, his breathing labored. The marshal studied him, then nodded. "Leander Stiles," he said. "Two hundred and fifty dollar reward."

The wounded man, his right shoulder black with infection, lifted his left hand, as if making some plea for help.

Silas started to speak, but heard a rock tumbling down the canyon wall above him, then another. "Rock slide," he screamed as the whole canyon wall seemed to be falling toward him.

CHAPTER 14

Sulky winced as he grabbed for a dead juniper bush that had taken root between two flinty crags. The big man had hurt him, more than anything since the grizzly bear, and the pain bit him with each deep breath. He inhaled slowly to delay the ache, but progress was slow and hard as he inched along a narrow ledge toward the canyon mouth where the shooting had been yesterday.

Three of the evil men had ridden away after the gunfire, so one man — the one he had shot with the arrow — remained. Sulky must be sure he was dead before he trailed the others.

And too, Sulky was curious about Bill Whitman. From all the shooting, the marshal and his deputy must have caught up with the evil men. The bad men would not have galloped away had they killed the deputy and his marshal, yet it was unlike

205

Whit not to pursue his prey. Sulky discounted that Whitman was dead because he was too mean to die.

"You too long carry grudge, Bill Whitman," Sulky said, his thoughts becoming words.

A slice of the ledge gave way under Sulky's left foot, his moccasin dangling for an instant in the air a hundred feet over the canyon floor. Tottering on the brink, he caught a deep breath, pain shooting through his chest, as his fingers crawled along the cliff face, feeling for a hold to stabilize him. They found a crack and slipped in it.

Sulky froze to the cliff and waited, fearing the narrow ledge beneath his feet would give way. Common sense said a fall would kill him, but Sulky felt within his soul that he should never die until Dawn had been fully avenged. If he fell, he would fly like a bird to safety.

But the ledge held and Sulky crept by the soft spot and studied the path before him. It gradually widened and then turned a bend which had covered his approach. Once around the bend, he would have a good view of the canyon mouth and the site of the fight.

Of course, Bill Whitman just might be expecting him, lying between two rocks with his carbine aimed at the ledge, just waiting to shoot Sulky and see if he could fly. Sliding his feet gently along the ledge as if it reduced his weight, Sulky rounded the bend and the ledge fanned out, giving him a wider path where he could cling to the early morning shadows and observe the canyon unseen.

Slipping into a shadow, he watched now, noticing five horses hobbled in a circle of rocks, a dead horse sprawled on its side in the middle of the trail and two men moving to his side of the canyon. Whitman was alive and walking! The deputy too. Sulky wondered why the marshal had given up the chase yesterday.

Sulky worked his way along the ledge, moving closer to them, clinging to the shadows and crouching low, in spite of the pain. He grabbed at his left side, excruciating to the touch, and wondered if he had a cracked rib. Whitman and his deputy moved among the rocks, working their way up the canyon face, but never looking toward Sulky. Sulky moved as fast as the pain would allow him, then reached a perch that offered a suitable view of the terrain below and he stopped, as much to ease the pain as to inspect the canyon. Studying the direction of their climb, Sulky let his gaze slowly crawl up the canyon side, finally spotting their destination. There just down the way from him on a level patch of ground lay a body. At least Sulky thought it a body until he saw it move. It was the man he'd shot with the arrow. He was still alive.

Sulky cursed in the language of the White Eyes.

Angered that the White Eyes still lived, Sulky slipped along the ledge until he found a wash where the flint hard rock had broken away and the tailings of eroded soil had formed a gentle incline that led toward boulders bunched like giant bird eggs balanced on perches undercut by the wash of erosion. If he could make it there, perhaps he could kill the wounded man after all. If he could make it to the boulders, perhaps he could send them tumbling down upon the wounded man and bury him so deep beneath the rocks that even the worms couldn't find him.

And if he killed Bill Whitman as well, it would be good, for Bill Whitman would surely kill him later, if he got the chance.

Making his descent, Sulky studied Whitman, noticing an awkwardness in his movements. Then Sulky spotted the bandage on the marshal's arm. That explained why he had not chased his ambushers, why he had not seen Sulky moving above him. A younger Whitman, even wounded, would've spotted his stalker.

Reaching the boulders, Sulky slumped over, his hands on his knees, each breath a bellows fanning the flame of pain within him. He hurt so much he wanted to lie down and sleep, but he knew he could never rest truly, not as long as Dawn's killers lived. Straightening, he arched his back against the stabbing rib in his left side, then peeked at the deputy and Whit meandering up to the wounded man.

If he could just get the rocks to budge, Sulky knew he could bury them all. He moved among the rocks as fast as his pained body would let him, pushing against one, then another, testing a half dozen before he found one that stood balanced upon a single pinnacle of dirt, eroded on all sides. It looked so easy that Sulky pushed it with his hands, but it held. He pounded on it with his fists and still it showed no signs of giving. Turning around, he leaned his back into it and pushed with his feet against a bigger rock behind him. He held his breath and shoved, shoved harder than the pain seemed it would allow. He grew faint and verged on passing out from the pain when the rock quivered, the width of a fingernail, no more.

Taking a deep agonizing breath, he shoved his feet again, the muscles straining from his toes through his thighs. Pressed against the roughness of the rock, the grizzly's scar sizzled under his shirt. The rock gave again, the width of a finger, then the width of a fist.

Then it gave way totally and Sulky pushed against nothing but air. He slammed into the ground beneath where the rock had been and cried out in pain, but the sound was lost in the noise of rocks crashing against one another, a clacking of collisions which quickly gathered into a great rumble lost in a plume of dust. Despite the pain, Sulky spun over to his hands and knees and watched, the rocks cascading away from him, toward the wounded man and Bill Whitman.

Sulky saw the deputy freeze, then yell out a warning and run. Whitman turned, then chased the deputy, both men scrambling down the slope like mountain goats. The boulders rained down toward them and they were still running when the dust and debris boiling up from the slide obscured his vision.

Knowing the cloud of dust would screen him, Sulky scrambled away, running as quickly as he could up toward the ledge that led to his hiding place. The cloud of dust was still settling when he stumbled up to the wide section of the ledge. He leaned back against the wall into the shadows and waited, watching intently.

Gradually, the dust evaporated like a fog and what he now saw was not what he had seen before. The whole side of the canyon had changed, debris washing all the way out to the canyon floor. Where the wounded man had lain was gone, or at least buried under a layer of rock. Half the men who had killed Dawn were dead now. The next three would be easier to kill because they were headed toward the sands, a great expanse of white sand between two mountain ranges. It was not an impossible trek across those sands, but Sulky would make it tortuous for them.

Then he saw a movement among the slide debris, the deputy standing up, then bending down beside him and helping Bill Whitman to his feet. Evidently, they had made it halfway down the slope, then hidden in a crevice, as the debris passed overhead. Whitman wobbled on his feet, steadied himself and touched two fingers to his nose, then swept his fingers away in an arc to his side. He did this three times and Sulky remembered this signal from the days they had scouted together, a silent sign they had used to communicate that the enemy was near.

Sulky nodded. Bill Whitman knew who had started the avalanche. Bill Whitman knew Sulky was up there, knew he was watching him, knew that they must encounter each other on down the trail and knew that one of them must die.

Sulky touched his two fingers to his nose and swept them in an identical arc to his side, once, twice, three times. "I tell you," Sulky said, "you too long carry grudge, Bill Whitman."

As he watched Whitman scanning the cliffs for him, Sulky recalled the trip that had changed his life, making him a legend among the Apaches for killing a grizzly bear with his hands and a knife and leaving him Bill Whitman's enemy for life. Having heard the Apaches were planning to avenge an attack on one of their camps by killing Whitman's wife and daughter, Sulky had slipped away from Fort Bowie into the land that was Apache and went to his warrior brother, beseeching him to spare Whitman's family, then threatening him with death if he didn't. His brother had promised to let them live. But his brother had lied. And figuring it so, for his brother had always lied even to his father about their runs as boys, Sulky had been hurrying back to the fort to warn Whitman when the grizzly bear had jumped him.

"You too long carry grudge, Bill Whitman," he said, then cursed with the best words in the language of the White Man and the Apache.

Below him now, Whitman seemed to understand he would not spot Sulky, so he turned away, his deputy following him to the canyon floor.

Sulky watched them gather their bedrolls, saddle two of the five horses, then turn the others free. Finally, Whitman mounted and started deeper into the canyon, the deputy trailing him. Whitman would follow the canyon, just as the evil White Eyes surely had, but Whitman didn't know the canyon. Sulky did. It cut through the mountain, then picked up a trail that ended at a great spring, the last good water before the sands and the wide stretch of misery between mountain ranges. Even if Whit got ahead of him now, Sulky would pass the marshal and the deputies by going over the mountains, avoiding the circuitous canyon trail, and waiting at the good water for the evil White Eyes.

When Whit disappeared around the bend

in the canyon, Sulky stood and stretched his arms, the pain in the rib still burning deep into his chest. Then he followed the path along the narrow ledge around the bend toward the den where he'd rested after his fight with the big man. There he gathered his weapons, his pouch and his deer stomach water bag and climbed gingerly on Ember. Bonita watched, then followed Ember as the stallion moved toward the trail. The stallion was frisky, anxious to gallop once they reached the trail, but Whitman was still too close for that and the jarring strides of the gallop would send throbbing pains down Sulky's side. Too, they would not follow the canyon trail for long, just until the canyon split into a vee, the main section veering away to the right, a nub of the canyon veering to the left and dead ending within pistol range of where the canyon split. But there, at the head of the box canyon, was a narrow path, wide enough for a man afoot to lead a horse up to the rim. From the rim fanned out a great mountain meadow which narrowed into a pass that provided comfortable passage over the divide and looked out over the great expanse of white sands.

Sulky fond the path badly eroded, yet passable and with patience he led the horses to the brim and onto the broad meadow. Before him the tall grass drooped under its own weight. It was a good land for grazing and here was a good place for what he must do. Reaching for Bonita, he grabbed her head and pulled her to him, stroking her and blowing a breath into her nostril.

He lifted his mouth to her ear. "This be your home," he whispered so the stallion wouldn't hear. "Take freedom and ride on the wind. You shall never have rider as beautiful and gentle as the one departed from us, so you shall never have rider again. Find a wild stallion, have many colts, eat the good grass and drink the cool water of the mountains."

Sulky pulled the halter over her ears. Bonita tossed her head as the halter came free. Sulky slapped her neck. "Go!"

She trotted a few paces, then turned to stare at Sulky and the stallion with uncertain eyes.

Sulky waved his arms at her.

Bonita tossed her head, then pranced a few steps away, stopping once again.

Sulky clapped his hands, "Mountains now your home."

Then the mare galloped around the meadow in gradually widening circles that led her in and out of the surrounding trees.

Dawn's spirit would celebrate Bonita's freedom.

Ember stamped the ground, pulling against the reins Sulky still held.

"No fellow," Sulky said. "You stay with me until all the evil White Eyes are killed."

Sulky crawled back upon Ember. His ache reminded him of his age, the stinging rib of his mortality and the dull pain across his back of the grizzly. And the grizzly reminded him of Whitman.

He whistled and Ember started forward into a trot, Sulky pulling up on the reins because the pain was still great. And they rode west, toward the good waterhole. To the north were waters bad for man or animal, but the evil White Eyes by the route they took would wind up at the good water hole. There, Sulky would surprise them.

By midafternoon, he had spotted the water hole. He hobbled Ember at a distance and carried his carbine and his antlered headdress among the broken cover of trees and rocks. And he waited. At dusk, three riders approached.

CHAPTER 15

"Dammit," Ben Bastrop shouted, standing up in his stirrups, "my horse's back is so galled, one of us is gonna be afoot. Dammit, Dummy, why didn't you put the saddle blanket on him?"

Dummy felt himself withering under Bastrop's hard stare. He had tried, but Ben would never believe him.

"Leave him be, Ben," Pete answered, a challenge as pointed as barbed wire nailed to his words. "He saddled three horses during the shooting. If it'd been you, you'd saddled yours and left us."

"Yeah, and we'd both been better off," Bastrop answered, chewing on a twig instead of a cigarette since he'd exhausted his tobacco.

Pete nodded. "I've been thinking the same thing, Ben. After we find water, Dummy and me are heading back."

"You said that before, Pete, before you

winged Whitman back there. You weren't gonna fight. Why'd you change your mind?"

"They shot at Dummy. I was protecting him, it had nothing to do with you," Pete answered. "We're still going back, make things right."

"You'll go back broke. I'm not splitting the money with you until Whitman's dead or we're shed of him," Bastrop said.

"Greed's your sin, Ben," Pete answered. "All that money in your saddlebag and you aren't within twenty miles of a good horse you could buy or even fresh tobacco."

Dummy realized Bastrop was studying his mount.

Pete noticed too. "You're not taking Dummy's either," he said, his hand sliding toward his revolver.

"Thought you were gonna demand a full share for Dummy so you could set him up in some lunatic asylum, Pete. You backing out on Dummy, too?"

Dummy didn't know what a lunatic asylum was and from the contempt in Ben's voice, he wasn't interested in learning.

"Ill gotten money's ruined my life. It won't ruin his."

Dummy wasn't sure exactly what Pete meant, but he did understand that the ten dollars Ben Bastrop had promised him for licorice didn't seem worth what he'd been through, the hard riding, the nights of bad sleep, the days of little food, the deaths of the others. He wasn't so sure he could ever enjoy the taste of licorice again.

Ben Bastrop shifted in his saddle and his horse shied away from his weight, then reared on its hind legs. "Let's ride 'fore my horse turns useless," Bastrop said, jerking savagely on the reins until the horse's head twisted brutally back.

Pete nodded to Dummy. "We'll ride to water, then we'll leave Ben and you'll never have to fear him again."

Dummy smiled. It was a pleasant thought, like a daydream that you thought would never come true and then one day it does. His horse fell in step beside Pete's. Bastrop's limped ahead at a slow pace and every time Pete's horse neared Bastrop's, Pete pulled up on the reins and let his horse graze a moment on the grass. Dummy followed suit. It was like Pete didn't want to ride in front of Bastrop, as if he might do something terrible to them. Dummy couldn't figure what it would be. Bastrop had all the money. All they had were their horses.

They had left the canyon behind earlier in the morning and now were topping a succession of dwindling mountains, each with less and less cover and each, Dummy thought, with fewer places for the deer on horseback to hide.

Finally, they topped a bald hill and Bastrop held up his hand. Here they could see for miles and Dummy gasped at the enormity of the world. It seemed to go on forever until the blue of the sky melted into the ground so nothing divided heaven from earth. Dummy wondered if they'd eventually ride into the sky. But between the sky and him lay a vast patch of white ground. He figured it was snow until Ben spoke.

"The sands, the white sands," Bastrop said. "That's where I'll lose Whit Whitman."

Pete laughed. "A blind man could follow your trail there."

"Only a fool would follow me!" Bastrop answered.

"That'd put two fools out there then," Pete responded.

Bastrop kicked his horse and started down the mountain. After he got a comfortable distance, Pete motioned to Dummy. "Don't get too close to Ben. His horse may go wild from pain."

Dummy figured Pete was as worried about Ben turning wild as his horse. Pete nudged his horse and it moved ahead, but Dummy stared at the white sands. Except for one lingering horror — the deer on horseback — he was glad Pete would be turning back from the sands.

"Come on, Dummy," Pete called gently and Dummy jiggled the reins against his horse's neck and the animal trudged ahead. Dummy rode with a great hunger, reminding him he had had no food all day. Pete no longer offered him dried apple slices so Dummy knew they were depleted, but knowing didn't stop the craving. He missed his ma's food and his stomach wished he'd never run away from home, but it wasn't easy to take his younger sister being smarter than him.

"Dammit, you two coming or just lollygagging around?" Bastrop yelled, twisting in his saddle, his mount tossing its head and kicking at the pain on its back.

"We're keeping our distance from your horse, she's too skittish when we're near," Pete said.

"Is it my horse or me, Pete?" Bastrop asked, easing back around in his saddle.

Pete spat at a bush, hitting the top leaf. "I've learned never to turn my back on you, Ben. Especially not when I've something you want."

Ben laughed. "I got the money." He patted the saddlebags and laughed again.

"But I've got a good horse and Dummy has a good one," Pete said, "and you'd gut either one of us for 'em."

"You're awfully suspicious of your brother."

"Stepbrother, Ben, and you'd steal our food if we had any."

"You're mighty harsh, brother, on a fellow sinner. For all that Bible reading you do, seems you'd made a better example of yourself."

Dummy saw Pete swallow hard and pull his hat down over his eyes, as if he were ashamed.

Pete nodded weakly. "I've known right from wrong all along, Ben, and I'm damn ashamed of what I've done. You never cared about right or wrong, just yourself."

Dummy knew right from wrong, or at least thought he did. It was right to hold the horses, but not to rob the train. At least that's what he had thought, but anymore he wasn't so sure, not with Pete nervous about his part in the train robbery. Pete was a decent man, but he'd done some bad things riding with bad men. Did that make him bad? Did that make Dummy bad? When he'd done bad at home, ma or pa would whip him and then he'd know. It was simple, but since leaving home he hadn't had any whippings, but he wasn't so sure he hadn't done anything wrong. It was so confusing that Dummy wished he could forget about it.

He would've considered it longer, but he noticed a change in his mount's step, a liveliness he hadn't felt all day.

"The horses smell water, Dummy," Pete said.

Dummy didn't see any and he turned to Pete.

Pete released his reins and let his horse follow the scent tickling its nose. "Go easy on the reins, Dummy, and your horse'll lead us to a cool drink."

Dummy nodded, wishing he could get something to eat too.

"If it's water," Ben called back over his shoulder, "this is where we split up, Pete, and I'm keeping the money, all of it."

Pete nodded. "I'll not deprive you of your damnation, Ben."

Dummy's horse topped a ridge and Dummy caught the glint of sun rays bouncing off a crystal surface. Water! He licked his cracked lips with what little moisture his tongue could muster. His horse jogged at a steady clip-clop down the slope toward the water which lay as motionless as a pane of glass. At the base of the slope, the horse shuddered and blew hard, its step faltering as its ears twisted forward toward the water hole. Dummy studied the indecisive country before him. It was neither mountain nor prairie, but a little of each, scrub pines mixed with piñon and juniper, tufts of mountain grass growing in the moist soil surrounding the water, ocotillo reaching skyward with its thorny tentacles from the drier soil inches away. Around the pristine pool, boulders clustered like giant marbles dropped from the sky.

Ahead, Bastrop's horse drove into the pool, taking long draws on the water.

"Dammit, Ben," Pete called. "Don't let your mount muddy the water 'fore we get a drink."

Bastrop laughed. "You could've ridden point, Pete, but you were scared to turn your back on me." Bastrop spit in the pool, lifted his leg over his saddle horn and slid off the saddle into water halfway up his boot. His horse, stung by the saddlesores, reared on his hind legs, flailing its forelegs against the sky. "Down, dammit, down," Bastrop yelled, jerking savagely on the reins, the animal's head twisting backward, until Dummy could see its bloodshot and dilated eyes. "Dummy's fault, this is," he said, spit-

224

ting into the pool again, "and it's slowing us down."

"You coming, Dummy?" Pete said with a glance over his shoulder. "Don't let him scare you."

Dummy nodded, but Bastrop did scare him. Without Pete, Dummy figured Ben would treat him as bad as he did his horse.

Pete pulled up shy of the water and let Dummy's animal catch up. Pete studied Dummy's snapping finger for a moment. "What's bothering you? Ben?"

Maybe, Dummy thought, but it wasn't just Ben. Still, Dummy made sure Pete's horse was between his and Ben's as they sloshed into the water and danced in its wetness.

"Hop down and take a drink, Dummy," Pete said, unstrapping his canteen from his saddle horn. "Fill this for me, would you?"

Dummy stood in his stirrups, studying the surroundings, then stepped off the saddle, jumping for the edge of the pool, stumbling on the uneven gravel bottom, then tumbling onto the grass carpet surrounding the water, the commotion spooking Bastrop's horse into rearing on its hind legs until Ben jerked its head down with the reins.

"You're plaguing me, boy," Bastrop called, a low growl, like a wolf's, in his throat.

225

"You're okay, Dummy," Pete said, his outstretched hand still holding his canteen. "Get a drink, then fill my canteen."

Dummy worked himself up on his hands and knees, crawling to the water's edge and lowering his head to the crystal surface. Dummy touched the water with his lips and caught his breath at the cool wetness, the tingle sliding down his throat with each swallow until he started to gulp the water down.

"Not so fast, Dummy," Pete cautioned. "Too much is bad for you so quick. Fill my canteen before you take another sip."

Studying the water, Dummy caught his reflection and smiled, thinking of his ma's hand mirror that had fascinated him so until he had dropped it, cracking its face, and his ma had scolded him never to use it again. He caught the canteen Pete tossed him. Uncorking it, Dummy poured the mouthful of water still inside onto the grass.

Dummy grabbed the canteen by its neck and submerged it in the edge of the pool, watching the bubbles boil from it until they trailed off into nothingness and the canteen sank from its fill. Dummy pulled the canteen out by its straps and tipped enough water from the neck until he could replace the cork. He handed it back to Pete, who retied it to his saddle, then dismounted, wading to Dummy's horse and untying his canteen.

"You'll need this full for yourself, Dummy," Pete said, his horse advancing to the middle of the pool.

"Care to fill mine, Dummy?" Bastrop called, the guttural growl of a wolf lingering in his words. "That's not much to ask of the fool that ruint my horse."

Pete coughed. "Fill your own, Ben. You've been hoarding yours and the two extra canteens for yourself."

"I plan to ride across the white sands. If you two are sprouting chicken feathers and giving yourselves up, they'll give you plenty of water in prison." Bastrop unsnagged the corks from his canteen trio and tossed them at the water's edge, letting them sink and fill slowly at his feet.

Dummy felt Bastrop's hard gaze and dropped back to his hands and knees to fill his own canteen, submerging it and bending over the water to drink at the bubbles rushing to the surface. The water bubbles tickled his mouth as he swallowed the water. It tickled so he was almost choked when a laugh came up as a swig of water was going down. He coughed, sputtered and caught his breath, staring at the water.

Then he saw it. Another laugh died in his throat.

There in the water, an apparition wriggled on the gentle ripples of the pool. Dummy blinked once, twice, three times and still it did not go away. In the reflection he saw crimson-stained antlers pointed right at him. His eyes lifted enough to follow the reflection which stretched across the pool. It was a deer, dressed in pants and standing on his two hind legs on a rock. Dummy raised his head, his gaze inching out of the pool and up a boulder on the opposite side of the pool. The deer that rode horseback stood with his back to the sun. Dummy wanted to shout a warning, wanted to scream, wanted to make a noise more than ever before in his entire life, but now the words were chained by fear between his brain and tongue. He watched, but the deer did not seem scared. Dummy reached for the pistol at his side, but his hand shook too much to pull it from his pants.

The deer's head twisted and Dummy froze as much as his shakes would allow him. He averted his gaze from the deer and studied the water by him. He grabbed the straps of the canteen and pulled it slowly from the water, thinking as he did of Pete's reading on David and Goliath, how David had flung a rock at the giant and killed him. Dummy gathered the canteen to him, stood up slowly and then instantly began to swing the canteen over his head as hard as he could.

"What the . . . ?" Bastrop shouted, then let the question die.

The canteen gathered momentum and Dummy released it.

"Get mounted, Dummy," Pete yelled.

The canteen bounced against the boulder at the deer's feet and the deer jumped from the rock at them, carrying a carbine.

Dummy splashed through the water for his horse, the animal rearing at his approach.

Pete dashed for the reins to Dummy's horse, snatching them from the air with snake quickness. "Hurry, Dummy," he shouted, jerking his pistol from its holster.

Dummy lunged for his saddle horn, stumbling and falling headlong into the pool. He came up spitting water, just as Pete fired a shot. The horse reared again, but as it came down, Dummy grabbed the saddle horn and shoved his foot in a dangling stirrup. He was half up when Pete tossed him the reins and the horse bolted out of the water, the air shaking with another shot, then reverberating with a scream of the walking deer.

His crazed horse dashed from the water, then circled as Dummy held one rein but could not reach the other dangling down from the bridle toward the ground. As he struggled for the other rein, he caught glimpses of the water hole.

Ben Bastrop had caught a horse, Pete's horse, and was jumping on top of it.

The walking deer charged into the pool toward Pete, but Pete fired and the deer tumbled headfirst into the water. Dummy could not figure if Pete's bullet had caught the animal or if it had just tripped. The thrashing of the water around the deer gave him doubts the deer had been shot.

Pete lunged for Ben's leg, but Bastrop was kicking the flank of the horse wildly as he raced by. Missing Ben's leg, Pete grabbed the oiled stock of his Winchester, the carbine flying from his hands and splashing in the water.

Dummy finally managed his reins and held up on his mount as Ben Bastrop raced by.

Pete yelled, "Ride, Dummy, Ride."

"No," Dummy yelled, the word surprising him.

Where the deer had fallen, the antlers slid away into the water and a man stood up. Dummy blinked, not understanding the transformation. The man bent over the water, shoving his hands beneath it, pulling up the antlers and flinging them aside, then grabbing for something else.

Ben's horse flailed its hooves toward the attacker, its eyes wide with terror now. Pete stumbled to the horse, leaped for its saddle horn, caught it. The horse whinnied and swung its legs around to strike its new tormentor whose weight was pulling the saddle down on its saddle sores.

The man still in the water raised his carbine, shook it of water and aimed at Pete. Dummy shuddered at the explosion of powder which engulfed Pete like a malevolent cloud.

But the horse was bucking so, the bullet must have missed for Pete still clung to its back. Then Pete fell forward over the animal's neck, grabbing the horse's mane. The horse settled for an instant, stepped toward the man leveling the rifle toward them, then dodged away and out of the water just as another shot rang out.

Dummy felt a flutter in his heart as Pete broke free and the horse dashed out toward him.

"Now ride, Dummy, ride hard," Pete yelled.

Dummy spun his horse around and

dashed away in the direction Bastrop had taken, charging headlong toward a downhill ridge. He heard another shot behind him and glanced at Pete, still astride the horse, but riding funny, tilting like a chair on uneven legs.

"Ride, Dummy," Pete repeated.

Dummy leaned back in the saddle as his horse hit the slope. Down the steep hill, Dummy could see Ben Bastrop riding away on Pete's horse, never looking back to see if he or Pete had survived.

Over his own labored breath, Dummy could hear the hooves of Pete's horse striking the rocky slope behind him. Once they got away from that deer or that man, whatever it was, Dummy longed for Pete to take him away from Ben Bastrop.

Dummy could hear Pete's horse gaining on him. He felt a grin working its way across his face. There was so much he wanted to say to Pete, but the words came so hard. Out of the corner of his eye, he saw the head of Pete's mount dipping up and down. When the horse drew even, Dummy turned. "Thanks, Pete," he yelled, but the words caught in his throat.

The saddle was empty.

Dummy glanced back over his shoulder. Behind him was nothing but rocky slope.

232

He stared at the saddle, noticed a smear of blood and felt tears welling in his eyes, then sliding in pairs down his cheek. Dummy cried. And cried again, the tears blurring his vision until he gave up directing the horse and let it run free rein.

The horse went down the slope, and up another until Dummy lost track of how long he had been crying. And every time he felt the tears were about to stop, he'd catch a glimpse of the horse loping beside him. And the blood on the saddle.

"Whoa!" came a cry and Dummy realized another horse had joined his and the riderless one. It was Ben Bastrop, grabbing the reins to the riderless horse, then to Dummy's.

Gradually, both horses slowed, then stopped, blowing hard and tossing their foaming nostrils from the hard run.

"Well, Dummy," Bastrop said, taking in the blood on the saddle. "You won't have Pete to look after you any more."

Dummy saw a smile uncover Ben's rotting teeth, but there was no mirth in Ben's deep eyes, just murder.

"I guess I owe my stepbrother thanks," Bastrop laughed as he unstrapped the saddlebags from behind the bloodstained saddle. "I'd left the money there for that

Indian, if he hadn't got my horse and followed us."

Bastrop pulled his pistol, cocked it and aimed it at Dummy's head. "Now you're gonna do what I tell you, boy."

Dummy nodded, bit his lip and closed his eyes.

At the explosion of the gun, Dummy screamed. He thought he'd been hit, but it was too painless. He heard a thrashing on the ground near him and his horse was jittery.

Dummy cracked his eyelids and saw the riderless horse twitching on the ground, blood streaming from behind its ear. Dummy thought he would be sick, until Bastrop jerked on his reins. Then he felt panic creeping up him like a shadow.

"Let's ride, Dummy," Bastrop said. "I've plans for you."

CHAPTER 16

Sulky scrambled from the water, shaking the carbine. The riders were getting away and he'd missed them all, at close range even. His labored stride carried him quickly to a waist high boulder and he dropped to his knee, propping his left elbow on the rock to steady his aim and pressing the carbine to his right shoulder, despite the pain.

There was little time. Two riders had disappeared down the ridge. The third, though, presented a solid target, even if his horse ran an erratic path.

Gritting his teeth against the recoil, Sulky's finger slipped next to the trigger. The rider rode into his gun-sights and he pulled the trigger.

"Aaagh," Sulky cried. The Henry kicked his sore shoulder like a strong horse. His whole right side blinked between numbness and excruciating pain, his eyes blurring for a moment, then clearing in time for him to glimpse the rider disappearing down the ridge. Sulky thought the rider swayed in the saddle, but he could not be certain.

Through teeth gritted against the pain, he whispered, "Evil White Eyes, even if you run forever, I follow. If you go into the sands, there you die. And Bad Teeth die last and die worst."

Sulky slowly pushed himself up from the boulder, lifting the carbine with him. He arose with the pain of a grizzly long dead and a man as big as a bear newly killed. "This body grow old," he said, "I old man, not warrior."

He lifted his still wet carbine and studied the beads of water dripping from it. Without oil, the carbine would quickly rust and corrode. Like his joints, the carbine would never again work as it should. The pain in his shoulder subsided, giving way to a dreariness that settled in his legs like a fog in a valley. He trudged over the grass to the water and sank to one knee, scooping water a handful at a time to his mouth. The water went down cool and sweet. He took his time drinking, never turning his back on the east for there somewhere Bill Whitman was gaining on him. And Bill Whitman would try to kill him.

Studying the pool, Sulky saw the carbine

the last man had pulled from the escaping horse and dropped in the water. His own carbine out of bullets, he waded into the water, picked up the Winchester and levered out seven cartridges. If he were a younger man, he would've kept the Winchester for future battles, but Sulky knew he had few left. As he let the Winchester slide back into the water, he studied the cartridges. They would work in his Henry. Loading the Henry with them, he noticed three canteens, their straps curled like snakes at the edge of the water, and he remembered the fourth the young one had thrown at him. With the evil White Eyes riding toward the white sands, the canteens could make a special torture on the burning sands. He gathered the three nearest canteens, dumping the water from them, then walked around the pool and picked up the fourth, emptying it as well.

Finally, he gathered the antlered head-dress which he had flung from the pool to the bank. He must carry it with him too so the evil White Eyes would know their killer. He draped the canteen straps over his left shoulder and moved back up the mountain to the spot he had left Ember hobbled among the grass.

"Belly full?" he asked. "Grass no good

where we ride."

The horse took tiny strides the limit of his hobbles to walk to Sulky. Sulky threw the antlered headdress over Ember's rump, spreading it out to dry under the dying sun. The canteens clattered as he slid them off his shoulder and hooked them over the antlers.

"I take you to water, give you plenty," Sulky said, stroking the Ember's neck. "Tomorrow I kill the other White Eyes."

Sulky untied the hobbles and tossed them over the horse's neck. Catching his breath, Sulky jumped on Ember, hitting the horse's back with his waist and sliding his cramping leg over the saddle, his foot brushing a couple of canteens as he did. They banged against Ember's flank and he danced away from their touch.

"Easy," Sulky said and nudged Ember with his right knee until the horse headed for the water hole. The horse cleared the ridge and stepped lively toward the water, the canteens bouncing noisily together. At the pool, Ember took great draughts of water and while he drank, Sulky untied the deer stomach he used for a canteen and lowered it into the water until it filled.

He remembered when Dawn would carry the water bag and fill it for him. And when she would bring herself softly to him and how she would soothe his aches and massage his back where the grizzly had ravaged him. Dawn was to have helped him through his aging years, but now she was gone, taking his son with her.

Pulling the bag from the pool, he allowed Ember a final swallow and then he pointed his stallion north. Daylight was dwindling, so he put Ember into a lope despite the dull throbbing it caused throughout his bruised body.

Gradually, a blanket of darkness was drawn across the land and Sulky rode from memory of a hundred times over these hills when he had hidden from cavalry. Eventually, he came across two sentinel rocks, standing at the entrance to a wide gully. A hundred paces back into the gully was the water pool Sulky sought. He dismounted, cross hobbling Ember so the horse might not follow him. It could mean death. Then he took the canteens and strode back into the gully.

Halfway into the canyon, he could smell the water, a fetid odor of minerals leached from the innards of the mountains behind. The odor reminded Sulky of a buzzard's den. With no natural means to protect its young, a vulture would vomit around its nest. Predators would give a wide berth to the buzzard because of the odor.

Then he heard the gurgle ahead where the water seeped from between the stones. He drew up beside the pool, uncorked the canteens and held them by the straps until they took on weight and quit bubbling.

Corking them, he made his way quickly back to Ember, glad to be away from the odor. He secured the canteens and un-hobbled Ember. He climbed gingerly back on his horse and angled away from the gully.

He rode with the night toward the sands. He stared back toward the ridge where he had jumped the remaining White Eyes at the good water hole. He thought he saw a flicker of light and he studied more carefully. He saw it again, a flicker that lingered against the darkness. A campfire.

Bill Whitman was camped nearby. Sulky fingered the bearclaw necklace around his neck. The grizzly might kill him yet with Whitman closing in. But first he must kill the evil White Eyes.

Then it wouldn't matter what happened.

CHAPTER 17

Darkness had set in, but a crescent moon at their back gave Whit and Silas enough light to travel. Whit swept his good arm toward a pile of rocks a quarter of a mile down the slope. "Water," he said. "Last good water before the sands."

Silas could just make out the outcropping of rocks.

Whit rubbed his wounded left arm which was leaking a clear fluid which scabbed through the shirt bandage. "Could be the Bastrops are there or maybe even Sulky," he said, releasing his arm as if it didn't pain him as much as the thought of Sulky.

"You still figure Sulky started the slide on us?"

The marshal spit a stream of tobacco juice into a bush. Even in the dimness Silas could see the fire burning in Whit's eyes. "I don't figure, I know, dammit!"

"Intuition?"

241

Whit slammed his right fist into his left palm, his wounded arm vibrating from the anger. He started a howl, then bit off its head with clenched teeth and swallowed it whole, almost without a sound. "Sulky pushed the rocks down on us, deputy!" Whit coughed.

"I didn't see him."

Whit took a deep breath, the air whistling through his teeth on the intake. "You don't see Apache unless they want you to."

Silas shrugged, unable to shake the notion that the marshal was more interested in catching Sulky than the Bastrops. "What'd Sulky ever do to you?"

Whit stiffened and Silas's flesh prickled with a chill not borne by the night air. The flame in the marshal's eyes flared like a fire doused with bad whiskey. The seconds seemed to crawl by on hands and knees as Whit pondered the question and the chill only grew. The marshal coughed again, but Whit knew he was only stalling.

"Sulky betrayed me. It cost me my wife and my girl."

As the marshal spoke, Silas noticed a softness he had never before detected in Whit's voice. Silas turned his head away, his emotions tangled in his discomfort for Whit. He cleared his throat. "The tintype, you and your family?"

Whit spit again into the juniper bush, hard words following on the tail of the tobacco juice. "What were you doing looking through my things?"

Silas caught his breath, stunned as much by the accusation as the sudden change of temperament. "I . . . I . . ." he stammered, then stopped, turning around square with the marshal, his wits coming back with his growing anger. He grabbed Whit by his bad arm, feeling Whit flinch from the sudden pain. "I got the whiskey and shirt to dress your wound. It just fell out of your saddlebag." Silas shoved Whit's arm away.

"You shouldn't have looked," Whit answered. "We best check out the waterhole."

"I'll go," Silas said. He trudged back up the mountain to where the horses were tethered and pulled his carbine from its saddle scabbard, knocking one of the small pieces of firewood loose from where he had tied several atop his bedroll.

The wood made Silas's horse nervous and Silas still angered about it. He'd captured the extra horse from the Bastrops, but Whit had ordered him to unhobble and release them after the marshal had picked out the best replacement mount for himself. So the horses had been turned loose and the extra saddles and gear had been left back in the rockslide canyon. Silas felt the anger welling in him. He could easily have tied firewood on their saddles and when the manhunt was over, the mounts and saddles would've made Silas some profit. But Whit said they must travel light and the extra horses would be a burden.

The wood would make a fire if they found any meat to eat. Whit had stared warily at the wood since Silas had started collecting it, but the marshal never said anything. Whit's wound was sapping his strength and without some nourishment beyond the tobacco he always chewed he couldn't continue his chase after the Bastrops. Or was it Sulky he really wanted?

Going back down the slope, he passed Whit. "Bring the horses when I call."

Whit grunted and each went about his task.

Silas moved from bush to bush, gliding easily toward the cluster of rocks, stopping frequently to listen. Behind him, he could hear the stamping and blowing of his own horses, but up ahead came only the sharp edge of night's silence slicing through the air. He moved on, gradually coming within a stone's throw from the rock cluster. He dropped to his knees, then slid down on his belly and waited. From this range, he should hear voices or sleeping noises. But he heard nothing at first, and started to move until the sound of something lapping at the water made him freeze on his stomach. It was an animal. Meat! He crept forward. Lifting his head, Silas saw the faint silhouette of a young buck against the western sky. Raising his carbine slowly so the deer would not detect him, Silas finally brought it to his shoulder. The gun sprang to life with an explosion of flame and noise and the buck fell dead at the edge of the pool.

Behind him, Silas heard galloping hoofbeats. Whit was charging in like the cavalry. Silas jumped to his feet, took off his hat and waved. "All's okay," he yelled, "All's okay, Whit."

The hoofbeats didn't falter until they were right upon him. Silas planted his feet and leveled his carbine at the shadowy rider in case it wasn't Whit.

"You fool," Whit yelled, "why you shooting if all's okay?"

"Meat!" Silas lowered his carbine, figuring if he held it in Whit's general direction too long, he might just be tempted to see how good the marshal was at stopping a bullet. "Meat!" he repeated. "I killed a buck."

Silas heard Whit spit again. "Now half of New Mexico knows we're here, not to mention the Bastrops," Whit answered.

"Not to mention Sulky," Silas said, knowing Whit wouldn't answer. "The other half of New Mexico'll know we're here when I build a fire."

Whit argued. "No fire tonight. We're too close to the Bastrops."

"If you don't get something to eat, help you mend all the holes the Bastrops put in you, this is as close as we'll get."

Silas walked out to the horses and took his reins from Whit, then led his mount to the water. The horse drank well, then Silas tasted the water, remembering none sweeter. Behind him, Whit unsaddled his horse first, tossed his bedroll down on the grassy bank and then hobbled the mount before letting it water. It was unlike Whit not to let the horse water first so Silas knew the wound was paining him more than he let on. As the horse watered, Whit threw his bedroll and fell upon it, Silas noting that Whit had not taken a drink unless it was from his canteen. Shortly, Whit was breathing heavily.

After letting his bay water, Silas unloaded his wood, bedroll and saddle, then started a fire and skinned enough of the deer to carve four steaks from its flank. The fire cast a golden glow around the camp and the pool was as still as a sheet of gold, the horses having given up the water for the new grass in the moist soil around it. The flames reached toward the sky while the wood beneath it cracked, popped and jumped from the heat and the smoke gave off pine's perfume, the aroma tickling Silas's nose and putting his stomach to jumping with anticipation.

He jabbed the steaks with sticks and roasted them over the fire. Soon the meat was blackened from heat and he could wait no longer. He pulled the sticks from the fire, setting Whit's aside to cool for a minute and attacking his with tooth and jaw, the sizzling meat scalding his tongue at first touch. Silas gobbled the first steak, then turned to Whit. "Meat's ready."

Whit answered with a labored snore.

"Dammit," Silas said, pushing himself up onto his legs, shaking them of their tiredness, but the exhaustion only settled deeper in his muscles. He moved to Whit's side, the flame of the fire casting his shadow across the camp. As Silas reached to shake Whit's shoulder, he caught the gleam of the fire on something at Whit's head. His hand reached for the source of the reflection, his fingers closing around a bottle, the same bottle he'd doused Whit's wound with. Now it was empty.

Whit coughed and Silas flinched, then caught the odor of liquor on the marshal's breath. Silas dropped the bottle and gently touched Whit's right shoulder. Before he could shake him, the marshal's right hand flew to his waist and returned quick as a snake with his revolver. Silas was looking at the single vacant eye that could blink him to eternity.

"Meat's ready," Silas said, his voice breathy with surprise.

"Never touch me when I sleep," Whit scolded.

"I called, but you didn't answer," Silas answered.

Whit grunted.

"I'll bring your meat?"

"No, I'll get . . ." Whit struggled to sit up, then stopped. "Okay," he said, collapsing back on his blanket.

Whit gnawed the first steak as Silas fetched water for his canteen. Whit ate quickly, then washed it down with fresh water, wiped his hands on his blanket, then scooted back under the cover and was soon asleep.

For a while, Silas gnawed on Whit's second

248

steak, then threw it on the coals. The cool had settled in, but the pool of water tempted Silas to bathe. He undressed and plunged into the water, gritting his teeth against the chill. The cold was exhilarating and Silas wanted to scream like a kid, the weariness in his muscles hiding somewhere within him. Silas waded to the center of the pool, the deepest part, and the water came to his waist. He was about to kneel down so the water would reach his neck and wash away more than a week of trail dust when his foot brushed against something stiff and un-natural on the gravel bottom. Squatting in the water, his hand followed his leg to his foot and touched the metal and wood that he knew by feel to be a carbine. He pulled it from the water, held it to the dark sky and couldn't tell much except that it was a Winchester. By the feel, he knew it hadn't been in the water long.

He tossed it to the grass to inspect in tomorrow's light. Silas submerged himself to his neck and enjoyed the wetness until the urge for sleep took hold. He emerged from the water, his flesh pimpling in the cool night air. He shook himself like a dog, grabbing his bedroll and pulling a blanket free to dry himself on. After wiping himself dry, he pulled on his britches, shirt and socks and arranged his sleeping gear near his pistol and carbine. Shortly, he was in bed and quickly the night closed in around him. Feeling clean, he rested well, except for the frequent squabbling among coyotes ranging uncomfortably close.

It all seemed so short a time until he heard Whit calling to him. What did the old fart want this late in the night?

"Silas," Whit called, "Silas."

Twisting in his blanket, Silas opened his eyes and he was surprised to see the sky a pale pink. Silas rubbed his fists at his eyes.

"Where'd the Winchester come from?" Whit asked.

Silas frowned, then remembered his bath. "At the bottom of the water hole."

"Hasn't been there long, has it?"

"Reckon it's one of the Bastrops?" Silas stood up and gathered his bedroll, observing Whit's already propped up against his saddle.

"Most likely," Whit nodded. "Somebody surprised 'em here yesterday, though this don't look quite like Sulky's handiwork."

"How's that?" Silas finished tying up his bedroll and stretched his arms.

"Sulky usually leaves a few more bodies around than this."

Silas shrugged, walked to the firepit where

only ashes and a piece of burnt meat remained. He picked up the slab of venison and offered it to Whit. "It's well done, but it beats nothing." When Whit waved him away, Silas started gnawing it. He grimaced at the bitter taste, but chewed the char anyway. "Where'd Sulky get his name? It Apache?"

"He never smiled. Soldiers took to calling him Sulky. He had an Indian name, but had to keep changing it."

"How come?" Silas strapped on his gunbelt, then picked up his saddle and marched to his horse.

"Apaches are given their names by others. When a namegiver dies, those named by him must change their names. Some Apache superstition."

Whit circled the water hole, working his way to a rock opposite the horses. There, he squatted down and picked something off the ground. As he walked back, he occasionally stopped to inspect tracks.

Silas was saddling Whit's horse for him when the marshal ambled back.

"We had a little fight here," the marshal said, holding an empty cartridge up to his nose. "Powder's still fresh. Best I figure, Sulky jumped them and ran them off west."

"Toward the sands?"

"Yeah, but there's something odd about it

251

all," Whit said. "The unshod tracks, Sulky's horse, head off to the north."

Whit jerked the cinch tight on his horse. "What do you figure?"

The marshal only shook his head. "There's no figuring Sulky." With his good hand, Whit scratched his forehead. "Like the time he brought the heads of his brother and uncle to Fort Bowie. He never said a word. At least that's what I was told. I was in the stockade at the time after a two-week drunk. He just dumped those heads out of a tow sack on the parade ground and rode away without saying a word. Why, he was still hurting from the bear mauling when that happened. I figured he'd died of that wound long before now."

Silas studied Whit. The paleness was leaving the marshal's face and Silas decided the marshal would survive his arm wound, though he was uncertain if justice were any the better for it.

Whit examined the Winchester on the grass, clamped it under his left arm and worked the lever several times without result. Then he tossed the Winchester back in the water. "Travel light on the trail," Whit said.

Instantly, Silas clenched his fists and gritted his teeth. He could've sold that carbine for a little money. Dammit, Whit hogging any reward money to himself was one thing, but cutting Silas out of any potential profit was another. His right hand flew up to his left breast and wrapped around his polished badge. He was tempted to jerk the badge off and throw it at Whit's feet.

Whit studied the empty hull he still held. "Sulky's Henry probably fired this one."

Silas stirruped, then lifted his leg over the saddle. He scanned westward toward the sands. Buzzards were circling in the air that way, waiting for them to ride away so they could attack the deer carcass by the water-hole.

The marshal took to his horse, climbing awkwardly into the saddle. He seemed to study north — the direction Sulky had ridden away in — then looked west, staring at the buzzards.

"Sulky may not have missed after all," Whit said.

Whit heeled his horse's flank and the animal started toward the rise that gave way to the slope. Whit stopped at the top of the slope and Silas rode up beside him. A body was sprawled across the ground midway down the slope.

Whit spoke. "Sulky got another one. May not be any reward by the time we catch up with him, but plenty of reason to jail him."

Silas had heard it before, he clucked his tongue and his horse started down the slope. Whit quickly caught up with him, then passed him. Whit was standing over the body when Silas reached him again.

"It's Ben Bastrop's stepbrother," Whit said. "He was just worth three hundred dollars."

"To you," Silas answered, the bile bubbling in his two words, but Whit ignored it.

"That just leaves Ben Bastrop, the big one. He's worth five hundred to me. Not bad pay for about two weeks' work?"

Silas shrugged. "You're forgetting the kid that ain't right in the head. He's still riding with Bastrop."

"Yeah, but he ain't worth anything."

Sort of like deputies, Silas figured, but he bit his tongue rather than put that thought in words.

Whit remounted and looked up at the sky. "The buzzards'll take care of him for us. Bastrop can't be too far ahead of us now. I figure this one died a little before dusk yesterday. If Bastrop rested the night, we may reach him by midafternoon."

Silas nodded. "With Sulky headed north, we might get Bastrop after all."

The marshal shook his head. "I got a feeling we'll run into Sulky, too."

Silas detected the glimmer of a smile in Whit's eyes, but not on his lips. "Intuition?" Silas asked.

"Intuition," Whit nodded and started down the slope.

CHAPTER 18

The boot dug into his shoulder blade and shoved him out of his slumber. Dummy rubbed his eyes. They still ached from all the crying. What would he do without Pete?

"Get your lazy tail up, Dummy," Ben Bastrop shouted, then punctuated his command by kicking Dummy's shoulder.

Dummy rolled out from under his blanket, shaking like a dog just climbing out of water. It wasn't the morning cool, but Ben Bastrop alone that sent a shiver down his spine as cold as ice. Ben kicked at his blanket, which flew up in Dummy's face.

"Don't," Dummy responded meekly. If only Pete were here, but he wasn't and never would be again.

Ben seemed to read his mind. "You don't have Pete to protect you any more, Dummy."

Dummy pushed himself to his feet, swaying dizzily for a moment as the blood seemed to rush from his brain, then gradually return.

Ben sneered and stepped at Dummy, lifting his hand toward him.

Gritting his teeth, Dummy half closed his eyes and waited for the fist he expected to slam into his jaw. Then he couldn't have been more surprised than if Pete had returned from the dead driving a locomotive pulling a load of licorice.

Ben put his arm around Dummy's shoulder. He drew him into his chest, not exactly a hug, but then closer to it than anything else.

Dummy flexed his arm to break loose, but Ben held him uncomfortably tight. Dummy looked up, staring into Ben's brown watery eyes.

"Maybe I've been too rough on you, Dummy," Ben said.

Dummy looked behind him, toward the direction he had last seen Pete, half expecting him to be approaching camp. Otherwise, why would Ben be so nice to him?

"Walk with me a ways," Ben said. "I want to show you something."

Ben's breath was as rank as spoilage and Dummy hated being close enough to breathe it, but Ben's grip was iron, his step solid. As they walked away from camp,

Dummy remembered how his ma would take a chicken from the rest, go behind the house and chop off its head with an ax. Dummy's finger started snapping and tears began welling in his eyes. He'd seen his mother ax a hen once and he could never forget it, the hen flopping about on the ground, strewing blood all over, flapping its wings as it tried to find its head. Dummy wondered if he'd jump around so much when Ben killed him.

Stopping a stone's throw from camp atop a little rise that sloped toward the west, Ben swept his arm at the horizon of blue mountains in the far distance. "Mountains, Dummy, mountains. You understand mountains don't you? Like where we've been the past week."

Dummy nodded.

"A long way to those mountains, isn't it?"

Again, Dummy nodded.

"You're pretty smart, after all, Dummy," Ben continued. "Now most of the way from here to there is sands, a desert. It's hot, there's scorpions and snakes out there, just waiting for someone to come along. That's where I'm headed, Dummy. Do you want to come along with me?"

Dummy couldn't understand why anyone would want to go out there into the sands.

He shook his head vigorously so Ben wouldn't make him go out there.

"Between us, we just have my canteen." Ben paused, the sneer skulking back across his face. "And I don't have enough water for you."

A terrible feeling crawled up and down Dummy's flesh like a thousand scorpions. His lips were parched and his tongue dry. He wished now he had never thrown his own canteen at the walking deer or Indian or whatever he was.

"What are we gonna do, Dummy? Any ideas?"

Dummy shrugged. Pete would have had an answer, but Dummy doubted he could ever come up with one on his own.

"I thought I might risk it across the bad desert and let you go back the way we've come," Bastrop said.

His finger snapping faster, Dummy flinched as if one of those scorpions had brushed him with its stinger. The deer on horseback was back there somewhere. He could never face that creature alone. His brain spun like the wheel of a runaway wagon as he tried to figure a way to tell Ben he was scared. At first he mumbled something which even he didn't understand. Then a single word, coherent and plain, dribbled out of his mouth.

"Deer!"

Ben nodded. "I know what you're 'fraid of, Dummy, but I've done some thinking about it. You're safer going back."

Dummy felt his brow sink. He didn't understand.

"See, this Apache, or this deer on horseback, he's never attacked us but where we are, not where we've been," Ben explained.

It sort of made sense to Dummy, but he wasn't sure. The deer had always attacked ahead of where they had been.

"If you go back, then the deer won't bother you. I'll head into the sands, the deer will follow me and you can ride back to water."

Yeah, Dummy thought, that would work. He could get a drink and not have to fear that deer — or Ben — any more.

"You think it's a good idea?" Ben laughed.

Dummy nodded.

"You're smarter than I've allowed, Dummy."

Not smarter, but wiser, like Solomon, Dummy thought, a smile easing across his face. Maybe Ben wasn't so bad a man after all. He wanted to tell Ben that, but those kind of feelings were too hard for words. Dummy just shrugged and Ben slapped him on the back, a little too hard, Dummy thought.

"We best be saddling up and readying to ride, Dummy."

Dummy grinned and fairly skipped back to the camp, Ben's enthusiasm lagging behind him. Dummy threw a blanket over his horse, then the saddle and cinched it up tight. That done, he rolled up his blanket, wrapping it all in Pete's yellow slicker. If he found Pete back on the trail, he would wrap him in the slicker so he would not get cold and the rain wouldn't bother him. Dummy wished Ben would remember the ten dollars he had promised him for licorice. Ben had the money to do it, Dummy knew, because he slept with the saddlebag of loot. But Dummy wasn't sure how to ask him about it, things like that being hard to put into words.

After tying his bedroll behind his saddle, Dummy unhobbled his horse and tossed the hobbles over the bedroll. Ben worked quietly, saddling his own horse. Dummy slipped his shoe in his stirrup and pulled himself astride his gray, the animal dancing beneath him. There was something he had to say, Dummy knew. The word was easy for most people, but hard for him to make his brain tell that to his tongue so his tongue could tell it to others.

At first, he mumbled and then it came out. "Bye!"

Ben turned around, laughing. "Yeah, Dummy, bye. You be careful and buy me a little time?"

Dummy frowned. How could he buy any time when Ben hadn't given him any money? It was hard to figure. If Ben gave him his ten dollars, he would try to buy him some, but he wasn't sure stores sold time.

"One more thing, Dummy," Ben started, "you got your gun?"

Dummy smiled. Sure he did. He pulled it out of his belt and offered it to Ben.

Bastrop waved it away. "No, you keep it. But if you run into that deer or any other riders, show 'em your gun so they know you're a big boy and have one."

He could feel his smile widening. He was a big boy now, going out on his own back into the mountains.

"Let me show you how to do it," Bastrop nodded. He put his hand to his revolver butt and jerked it from his belt, quick as a snake striking. Shoving his revolver back in its holster, he motioned to Dummy. "You try it."

He stuck his pistol under his belt, held his hand out to the side like Bastrop had done, then dropped his hand to the gun butt, finally jerking it free from the stubborn belt.

Bastrop laughed. "That's it, Dummy, you just do that to anybody you meet."

Dummy felt so good, like when his ma used to say nice things about him. Why hadn't Ben acted this way before Pete was killed? So much didn't make sense, but his ma always taught him to treat people nice when they were nice to him. He had something else to say. It was up there, rolling around in his brain, like a loose marble in an empty freight wagon. Dummy caught his breath and squirmed on the exhale as he tried to free them, but the words missed his tongue the first time. He sighed, gathered in another breath and tried again. And then the words burst from his mouth as fast as quail flushed from under prickly pear.

"Thanks, Ben." Dummy was proud of himself.

Ben laughed and motioned with his arm to the mountain. "Go on, now!"

Dummy's chest swelled with pride as he turned his horse around, slapped the reins against its neck and pointed it toward the mountains. He had finally made friends with Ben.

And Ben was surely happy because Dummy could still hear him laughing heartily for a long way.

And when the laughter finally faded into his memory, Dummy never felt so lonely in all of his life. The sky was big, the mountains ahead were tall and he was thirsty.

Gradually, the hills steepened and the sun grew hot and a drink seemed a pleasure he would never again enjoy. The hills were ragged with gullies and eroded ditches forking out in spiderwebs before him. Into each gully and each ravine he looked for water and in each he found none.

And when he stopped in front of a ravine forking out from a tall hill, he froze in his saddle.

Not twenty motionless paces from him was the deer on horseback. He blinked his eyes and could see that it was really a man wearing a deerskin draped over his head. And Dummy saw something else. On a stretched bowstring, an arrow was aimed right for his heart.

Never had the world seemed so quiet.

Ben had tricked him!

CHAPTER 19

Spasms of pain shot up Sulky's shoulder as he pulled against the bowstring. It would've been simpler to use his pistol, but Bill Whitman was closing in on him. A pistol would make noise and tell Bill Whitman just how close he really was.

Now the rider opposite him just stared wide-eyed. Sulky had never seen a white youth like this. His head was misshapen, his eyes, nose and mouth pressed between an oversized jaw and forehead. His front teeth jutting out over his lip reminded Sulky of a squirrel. And when his eyes blinked, they blinked wide with fear. They were the eyes of a baby cottontail trapped by a predator. The youth's height was man-sized, but his eyes brimming with the cottontail terror suggested he was little more than a child. He wasn't right, this man-child.

Sulky watched the youth's hand slide from his reins down to his thigh, then up toward

265

his belt where the butt of a pistol poked above his britches. The youth's fingers wrapped around the butt of the pistol, his eyes never leaving Sulky's, then jerked at the gun, stuck in his britches. Sulky pulled back on the bowstring, despite the pain, waiting for the pistol to break free, but the gun seemed to want to stay.

The youth mumbled something that Sulky could not understand and the gun came free. Sulky flinched, but held on to the bowstring, its deadly load still aimed at the youth's heart. His fingers grew sweaty and he knew of no logical reason to wait, except that he was fascinated by the youth's awkward appearance, his awkward defense and, most of all, his child-like bravery.

The gun came clear.

Sulky kneed Ember's side and the horse danced away.

The youth swung the gun in an unsteady arc toward Sulky.

Sulky measured his own aim.

The youth's lips, then his whole jaw began to quiver. A pained look of disgust passed over his face like a cloud over the sun. His eyes widened beneath his low brow and his whole face seemed to convulse with muscles he couldn't control. His lips spread apart and his eyelids closed tight.

"Bang," he yelled.

Sulky adjusted his aim and released his bowstring.

His arrow sliced through the air, straight at its target.

The youth screamed when the arrow buried its head in the ground at his horse's feet. The horse reared up on its hind legs, the youth dropping his pistol as he grabbed for the saddle horn, his reins falling free. The horse punched at the air with his forefeet, then landed at a run, the youth yelling as he grabbed with his free hand for the reins. The horse bolted away.

Sulky kneed Ember hard and the black stallion shot out of the gully after the runaway. Ember took great, sure strides while the youth's horse seemed as nervous as him, running erratically away. Quickly, Sulky was beside the terrified horse and rider. Leaning over in his saddle, Sulky swooped up the loose reins and jerked on them, the horse tossing its head against the reins, then gradually slowing, Ember's stride decreasing with the other animal's until both had stopped, blowing and stomping from the short run.

Across from him, the youth trembled until Sulky feared he would fall from his horse. The youth's lips quivered and his face muscles seemed to contort from an additional strain.

"Thanks," he blurted out.

Sulky nodded.

Then the youth surprised Sulky. He lifted his hand and touched Sulky's face, then the antlered headdress. He grabbed an antler and tugged on it until the headdress almost slid from Sulky's head. He laughed a nervous laugh.

Sulky had vowed to kill the men who had molested Dawn, but this was not a man. He was but a child, even if in a young man's body. This one could never have harmed Dawn and Sulky would not harm him.

"Come," Sulky ordered, handing the youth the reins to his mount. Ember led the way back to the gully and as the youth's horse drew near, Sulky jumped from his mount at the arrow embedded in the earth and the nearby revolver, landing with a thump and an agonizing blast of pain in his shoulder. He bent over and retrieved the youth's revolver. He studied it, then looked at the youth, then the revolver again. The pistol had no trigger, and no hammer. And even if it did, it was empty even of spent hulls.

"No protect from gun," Sulky said, but the youth didn't seem to understand. Sulky took his own pistol from its holster and offered it to the youth. "One bullet, gun works, better to protect."

The youth shook his head. His whole face seemed to tremble as he answered. "No."

Sulky offered him the useless gun and the youth smiled and took it, shoving it back in his britches. Sulky pulled his water bag from his saddle and held it to the youth's mouth. "Drink!"

The youth grabbed the container and partook vigorously.

"Two men trail me," Sulky said, pointing to the east. "Ride toward mountains. Two men come this way. They help you."

The youth nodded as he returned the water bag and then he reached down toward Sulky, his fingers touching Sulky's cheeks, then crawling up his face to the antlered headdress. He made a strange noise that teetered between a laugh and an attempt to say something.

Sulky pointed toward the east. "Ride."

Again the youth nodded and reined his horse around. He nudged his mount with his heel and the horse started at a walk, then a lope. Once the youth looked over his shoulder back toward Sulky and Sulky thought he detected a smile.

Watching until he disappeared over a hill,

Sulky climbed wearily aboard Ember. The man with bad teeth was the only one left to settle with and he would not be far ahead, Sulky thought. Sitting in the saddle, he noticed the arrow still in the ground. He would've retrieved it, except that it hurt to dismount.

The sands were ahead and that is where he would catch the man with bad teeth. "Run, Ember, we've a man to kill." Sulky nudged the stallion with his knee and the horse broke into an easy lope.

By high sun, they were well into the sands. By then, Sulky had spotted the man with the rotten teeth.

Sulky worked himself within rifle range and pulled his Henry. He had only the seven bullets he had taken from the carbine at the waterhole, but they'd do. Atop a tall dune, Sulky held Ember up and pressed the butt of the carbine hard against his shoulder until he gritted his teeth from the pain. Aiming at the horse, he squeezed the trigger and screamed at the instant agony, running like molten lead through his shoulder and torso.

On the opposite dune, the man with the bad teeth fell beneath his horse.

For a moment, Sulky's vision was blurred from the pain, then everything came back into focus. The man with the bad teeth was shooting at him with his revolver, but the distance was too far for the bullets to be a threat.

Sulky studied his enemy who finally realized he was wasting ammunition. The man with the bad teeth abandoned his still twitching horse and ran over the top of the dune out of sight.

"By sundown, evil White Eyes, you die," Sulky called. "By sundown, Bad Teeth, you die."

CHAPTER 20

Whit stood in his stirrups, then Silas saw the rider. Coming slowly over a hill toward them, the rider sat stiffly in the saddle, a slender wisp of a man too small to be Ben Bastrop.

"We've got company," Whit said, settling into his saddle.

Silas could see that. He clenched his fist around the reins. He saw lots of things that Whit wouldn't acknowledge. Like a mile back down the trail, he'd picked up Sulky's tracks where they had fallen in behind the tracks of the two remaining Bastrop riders. Whit had missed it or surely he would have noted Silas's sloppy tracking.

"How do you figure it, Silas?" Whit asked, as he fitted the reins in the hand of his wounded arm and flexed the fingers on his gun hand.

Dammit, Silas thought, here it comes again, Whit poking around for a soft spot like a coyote gnawing on a carcass for enough flesh to sink his teeth in and rip from the bone. He'd show him this time. "Must be the kid that ain't right in the head, but I can't figure how he got past Sulky."

Whit clucked his tongue. "Well I'll be damned, Mr. Deputy," he answered, "I'd a sworn you had missed Sulky's tracks back there. Guess I might be able to make a deputy out of you yet."

Unlikely, Silas thought.

"But it don't make sense, Silas," Whit mused, "him getting by Sulky. Sulky wants the hide of everyone who had a hand in his squaw's murder."

Silas cleared his throat. "Kid didn't have nothing to do with it, I bet."

Whit shrugged. "Sulky don't know that and don't care."

"Reckon the kid got Sulky?"

"Hellfire and brimstone, Silas, Sulky's Apache. No way in heaven the kid's gonna get Sulky. I'm the only one within a hundred miles smart enough to get Sulky."

Silas shrugged. "I thought we were after the Bastrops?"

"And Sulky! You're forgetting he stole our horses."

"He hobbled them so we could catch up."

Whit spit at the ground. "He pushed the

canyon down on us, dammit."

"I didn't see him."

"That's why you're the deputy and I'm the marshal. He tried to kill us and I'm gonna take him back for charges." Whit held out his arm. "Whoaa," he said. "We'll wait here for the kid. Could be a trick."

Silas studied the rider, nodding to himself that it was the dumb kid. His horse was poor stock, fagged out by the hard ride on the outlaw trail. From the kid's misshaped head, Silas couldn't tell if he had yet seen them for his eyes were deep set between a broad forehead and a curving jaw.

Glancing toward Whit, Silas noted the marshal was still wriggling the stiffness out of his fingers. Must be more of the marshal's damn intuition, Silas figured. Why else would the marshal be playing this like it was Ben Bastrop riding up as mean as if he had a hot ember in his boot?

"Take it easy, Whit. It's just the kid."

Whit sent a stream of tobacco juice flying on the downside of the hill.

The kid was at the bottom of the hill, starting up.

"Hello," Silas called and the kid glanced up.

A smile fluttered across his odd-shaped face. For an instant. Then his hand fell

274

down to his side.

"He may have a gun," Whit whispered, his loose fingers taking roost on the stock of his revolver.

"Easy, Whit, he's just a kid."

Silas touched his knee to his mount's side, hoping Whit wouldn't noticed he'd prodded the horse. The horse tossed its head, then started down toward the kid. Behind him, Silas heard Whit slap his reins against the neck of his mount. Dammit! This was one time Silas figured his sense was better in handling the situation than Whit's damn intuition. For the first time since Zack's death, he felt a kinship with someone — the kid. The kid was riding away from a bad situation and Silas figured he should too. The odds would be one to one now, Whit against Ben Bastrop or Whit against Sulky. Whit could fend for himself. The kid couldn't.

"Hello," Silas repeated when his horse came within twenty paces of the kid's. Whit reined up beside him.

The kid nodded, then mumbled something that came out as grunts and snorts. His right hand fell to his belt.

"No," cried Silas.

The kid's horse shied away from Silas's mount, turning his side to Whit.

275

Silas saw the butt of a revolver tucked in the kid's britches, beneath his belt.

"Don't do it, kid." Silas caught Whit out of the corner of his eye, the marshal's hand deadly still on his own revolver. "Don't, Whit."

The kid's fingers wrapped around the revolver handle and the pistol started sliding up and out of his britches.

Silas heard a growl in Whit's throat. He heard the rush of metal sliding out of oiled leather.

The kid's gun cleared his britches and started up in an arc toward Silas.

At that instant, Silas heard the click of Whit pulling the hammer back on his revolver. Silas twisted in his saddle, leaning over and stretching out as far as he could, swatting at Whit's revolver.

It was out of the leather, in one instant still pointed earthward, in the second instant aimed at the kid.

A giggle wrenched itself free from the kid's mouth.

Then Whit's gun exploded.

Silas tumbled from the saddle, his boot hanging in his stirrup, his frightened horse bolting away from Whit's smoking revolver. Silas felt the earth bounce up to meet him, then himself plowing through the rocky

276

ground a dozen paces before Whit grabbed the horse's reins and held him up. Silas reached for the stirrup and jerked his boot free, then scrambled to his feet and raced to the kid, spread-eagled on the ground, a crimson stain spreading across his right chest.

"Dammit, Whit, he's dying."

Silas knelt beside him, cradling the kid's head in his arms.

"He pulled a gun, Silas, you saw that. He might've killed you, if you hadn't ducked."

Then Silas saw the gun, still clasped in the kid's right hand. Silas caressed the boy's cheek, then reached for the kid's gun hand and pried his fingers from the gun butt. He studied it a minute, looked over his shoulder and threw it at Whit. "Look at it, dammit," Silas yelled. "It's empty, no trigger, no hammer, a toy at best."

"How was I to know?"

"Your damn intuition, that's how," Silas shouted. "Toss me my canteen."

"Don't be wasting your water on a dead man."

"He isn't dead! My canteen, Whit, or I'm getting it myself."

The kid tried to speak and with the mumble came a pink foam, spilling out over his lips.

Silas stroked his cheek. "It's okay, son. Your pain'll be over soon."

Whit rode over and dropped the canteen by Silas. "What he drinks'll be all the less you have in the sands."

"I'd rather die of thirst in that hell than live in Satan's hell with this on my conscience," Silas shot back.

Whit jerked the reins on his mount and rode away.

Lifting the canteen to his teeth, Silas bit the cork free and spit it out. He held the canteen to the kid's parched lips, letting a little slosh out on the swollen and cracked flesh. The kid's tongue licked at the moisture.

"Your name, kid, your name?"

He lifted the mouth of the canteen until a trickle of water drained into the kid's mouth. The kid's breath was irregular and had the wheezing sound of a bellows with a hole in it. The water gurgled in his mouth.

"Your name?"

The kid's swollen lips lifted at the corners. He whispered something indecipherable, then took a deep breath which he could not hold for it escaped out the hole in his lung. He sighed and took another great breath, his face contorting. "Dum . . . my," he rasped out.

"No, your real name."

The kid lifted his head at the canteen for another sip of water, the gurgling sound increasing as he took on the liquid.

"Your real name?"

A cold shiver wracked the kid's body from head to foot and his head shook, but Silas could not tell if that was his answer or just a symptom of dying.

"Your real name, so I can tell your folks?"

This time the kid's head shook mightily. "No," he wheezed, the hole in the bellows sounding bigger, "t'would . . . sh . . . sh . . ." he gurgled, "sh . . . shame ma."

Then his head went limp in Silas's hand, a final gasp and a pink mass of bubbles foamed out his mouth. The kid was dead.

Silas lowered his head to the ground, then bent his own in a silent prayer. Done, he corked his canteen and stared at the kid's innocent face. He was still kneeling when the marshal rode up with the kid's gray.

"Unsaddle the kid's horse, Silas, and we'll turn him loose. Sulky and Ben Bastrop can't be too far ahead."

Silas stood up, his feet spread, his knotted fists planted on his waist. "Not this time, Whit."

Whit sputtered tobacco juice for an instant. "What do you mean?"

279

"We've left the others to the varmints, but they were mean men. The kid wasn't."

"We'll lose time."

"I bury the people I respect," Silas said.

"You didn't know him, so how could you respect him?"

Silas lifted his hand to his badge, thumping it with his thumb. "If you don't wait, only this badge will accompany you. And when I'm done, I'm taking the kid's horse with me."

Whit nodded and turned his horse away, muttering "Hellfire and brimstone."

Silas went to his horse, untied his saddle bag and pulled a tin plate from inside. He'd used it to dig a shallow grave for Zack. Now he would dig one with it for the kid who called himself Dummy. It wouldn't be much of a grave in this hardpacked earth, but at least in death he might have a dignity denied him in life.

CHAPTER 21

Whit dismounted over the carcass, pulled his hat from his sweat-soaked hair and swiped at the perspiration on his forehead with the shirt sleeve of his good arm. He stared at the western sky where the sun blazed white hot over the sands. Jerking his hat back down to his ears, Whit studied the horse.

"Dead maybe three hours," he said. "It's hard to tell in heat like this." Whit looked up at the sun again, then bent over the dead animal, untying the saddlebags and tugging the bottom side from under the horse's flank.

Silas looked west where the ridge of mountains shimmered in the heat like blue ghosts, then at the tracks leading in that direction — a set of hoofprints following the impression left by boots. "How far you think Bastrop'll make it?"

"As far as Sulky wants him to."

"He could've killed him here."

Whit opened up the saddlebags and whistled. He glanced up at Silas. "What you say?"

"Why didn't Sulky kill him here?"

"He's Apache. He wanted to torture Bastrop. Can you think of anything worse than fleeing across the sands, knowing an Apache'll kill you if thirst doesn't first?" Whit stuck his hand in the saddlebag. "Bastrop left in a hurry, otherwise, he wouldn't have left his canteen and this." Whit pulled a bundle of greenbacks out of the saddlebag and held the money over his head like a trophy. "Looks like most of it's here."

"We never gave them time to spend much of it," Silas said.

Whit tossed the saddlebags across his saddle horn and then retrieved the canteen, uncorking and taking a long sip from it. Silas waited a moment for Whit to offer him some for the marshal surely realized Silas was low after giving the kid water. But the marshal corked the canteen and hooked it over his saddle horn.

Silas turned his horse from Whit and headed deeper into the sands, following the trail of the man afoot and his mounted tormentor. He rode with a bitterness in his throat that came from more than the gall of thirst. Several times he glanced down at his shiny badge, catching its glint from the sun, wondering why he had ever taken up with a marshal that kept his tarnished badge hidden beneath his vest. Behind him, Silas occasionally heard the dry squeak of Whit's saddle leather and the sporadic noises of his horse.

As he rode, he lost track of time because the minutes seemed to flatten out in the heat and stretch an hour into a day. When the sun was two fists above the distant mountains, Silas spotted a man on horseback, trailing another man on hands and knees.

Whit must have seen them about the same time for Silas heard him slap the animal into a trot and shortly the marshal was beside him. "Now we've got Sulky!"

"I thought we were after Ben Bastrop."

They were maybe a half mile away, but Sulky, who had not turned around, was touching his hand to his face and sweeping his arm out away from his body, three times.

"He's seen us," Whit said. "Be careful from here in."

Silas studied Whit and the crooked curve of a smile across his lips. Silas had never before seen even the hint of a smile on Whit except in the cracked and faded tintype.

Now it gave him an uneasy feeling in his gut.

In a matter of minutes, Silas drew up his horse opposite Sulky and the now prostrate Ben Bastrop, his face blistered from the sun, his lips cracked and bleeding, his eyes wide with fright, his clothes ragged from his ordeal. And all the time, Ben Bastrop stared at the four canteens hanging from Sulky's rawhide saddle.

Across his saddle and pointed at Bastrop, Sulky held a carbine. The antlered head-dress with deerskin draping down his neck and shoulders protected Sulky from the sun.

"You come after me," Sulky said, unhooking the four canteens and tossing them halfway between his horse and Bastrop. Wild with thirst, Ben scurried on hands and knees to the canteens. With snake-like quickness, Sulky shoved the carbine to his shoulder and fired, the sand splattering an inch ahead of Bastrop's reach. Bastrop collapsed on the hot sands.

"No more of that, Sulky," Whit said, his fingers wiggling dangerously close to his holstered revolver. "I'm here to take you to jail."

Sulky spit toward Whit's horse. "You lie. You're here kill me. I'm here to kill evil White Eyes, man who killed my squaw."

284

Silas saw Whit's eyes narrow with danger. "You could've saved my wife and child, many years ago," the marshal said.

"I try," Sulky said. "Learn about plan, come to warn you. Grizzly attack me."

"You could've warned me, Sulky."

"At fort, some say I did."

Silas glanced from Sulky to Whit and back, noticing that Bastrop was inching toward the water canteens.

Whit failed to answer Sulky.

"At fort, some say I warn you."

Whit jerked his revolver from his holster, pointing it at Sulky.

"Just a minute, Whit," Silas called.

"You stay out of this, deputy."

"At fort, some say I warn you to bring wife and child to fort."

"You were out of your head."

"Some of the time, Bill Whitman, but I tell you and you not listen, not bring wife and child to fort."

"You're lying, Sulky. Now I'm gonna avenge their deaths."

"You can't, Bill Whitman. I have done so. I killed the murderers."

"I don't believe it," Whit shouted, cocking his revolver.

"You in stockade but you hear I left their heads on parade ground at fort. I kill them for what they did."

"Your brother and uncle?" Whit asked, disbelief ringing in his voice

Sulky nodded. "They kill wife and girl child of man I called friend. That man change. He no longer friend."

Silas saw Bastrop lunge for the canteens, grabbing one and jerking the cork free.

Sulky pulled the carbine up to his shoulder, swinging it toward Bastrop. Before Sulky could take aim, Silas heard the explosion of Whit's pistol and the thud of a bullet. Sulky pulled the carbine's trigger and the bullet coughed sand wide of its target. The recoil of the carbine knocked it from Sulky's hands. Sulky's wide eyes looked down at his ribs, a crimson spot growing on his shirt, then he clutched the bearclaw necklace around his neck.

"Grizzly finally kill me," he called, his voice still strong. He tilted in the saddle, his antlered headdress sliding off. Then Sulky toppled down atop it.

Silas jumped from his saddle and fell to his knees by Sulky, lifting the Apache's hand, but the life was gone. Silas heard Bastrop beside him gasping for breath as he fumbled with one of the canteens.

"You killed him, Marshal," Silas said, pointing his finger at Whit's chest.

"He was about to kill my prisoner, a man with a five hundred dollar reward on his head," Whit shot back.

Silas laughed. "No, Marshal, you blamed him, didn't you, for your failure to save your wife and child? What happened to your intuition. Damn you."

Whit lowered his head.

"Damn you," Silas repeated, then turned to Bastrop, who was pouring the water down his throat faster than he could handle it. The water gushed out the corners of his mouth and down his face and onto his clothes and the sand. Silas grabbed for the canteen and jerked it away, but it was empty now. "Easy, fellow, too much'll make you sick."

Bastrop grabbed another canteen and began sucking it dry.

"Hold on, fellow," Silas cautioned.

"Let him be, deputy," Whit called out. "Let him drink enough to make him sick. He'll be easier for us to handle on the way back, make it simpler for me to get the five hundred dollar reward on his hide."

Silas stalked away from Bastrop, grabbed the reins of his horse and led him to Sulky's stallion, taking his reins as well. Noting the water bag, Silas untied it and drank of the warm water. It felt good as it rolled down his throat and sent an exhilarating rush through the rest of his body.

Still on his knees, Bastrop threw aside the second canteen and reached for the third, but he teetered off balance and fell to the ground, his nose parting a space in the sand.

"Get up," Whit commanded, but Bastrop didn't move. Whit, still holding his revolver, fired a shot beside Bastrop, scattering sand across him. "Hellfire and brimstone, get up," he called again, but Bastrop lay motionless.

Silas moved to the outlaw's side, grabbed his fleshy shoulder and pulled him over. His eyelids were wide open, but his eyes had rolled up and Silas saw only their whites. Silas felt Bastrop's wrist. No pulse. "He's dead," Silas said, dropping his hand and reaching for another canteen. Uncorking it, he lifted the canteen to his lips, then pushed it away as the fetid smell of its contents brought tears to his eyes.

Then he giggled, slightly at first, then louder until his whole body convulsed in laughter. "There went your reward, Marshal." He held his side against the ache of his great laughter. "Sulky had poisoned water in the canteens. Sulky was smart enough to kill Bastrop after you'd killed him." Silas laughed again, then fell instantly silent at the retort of Whit's pistol. The marshal had shot the dead Sulky again.

Whit was crazy, Silas thought, but he didn't care. "There goes all your reward money."

Whit lowered his revolver to its holster, then turned his gaze hard on Silas. "Nope."

Silas felt his hand slip down to his revolver, his blood suddenly as cold as the ice in Whit's voice. "What do you mean, Marshal?"

Whit opened the flap on the saddlebag draped in front of his saddlehorn. The bags had been Bastrop's. "The reward money, Silas. Railroad company won't pay without bodies. Prentice, Pete, Leander, Claude, the rewards on them total a thousand and fifty dollars. On Ben Bastrop, there's another five hundred. That's fifteen hundred and fifty dollars reward money that's mine. This way, I get my money, we return the rest and save the railroad and myself a lot of paper work." Whit thumbed through bills until he counted out fifteen hundred and fifty dollars. He pocketed his reward and returned the rest to the saddlebag.

"It's not the law, Whit. It's not the law," Silas replied, standing up and leading both horses by Sulky.

"I'm the law, deputy. I'm the law in these parts."

"If you're the law, why don't you ever wear your badge where folks can see it?" Silas asked, bending over Sulky, grabbing him by the shoulders and draping his lifeless corpse over his horse.

"Too good a target for outlaws aiming at my heart."

Silas laughed as he shoved Sulky's body across his black stallion. "Your heart's too small for a bullet to find." Silas stepped into his stirrup and mounted quickly, grabbing the reins to Sulky's horse. Silas jerked the badge from his shirt and tossed it at Whit, the marshal batting it to the ground with his injured arm. "I don't want any more of your law, Marshal." Silas tapped his horse's flank with his heel and the animal moved ahead, followed by the black stallion.

"With time, you'd have made a good deputy, Silas," Whit called. "Where're you heading?"

"Back to the mountains to bury Sulky."

A LARGE PRINT EDITION

NEW MEXICO SHOWDOWN
Preston Lewis

The Bastrop gang murders and plunders its way across New Mexico Territory, pursued by renegade Apache Sulky, who has vowed revenge. The law compels Marshal Bill Whitman to chase the outlaws as well. Friends long ago, Sulky had led death to Whitman's door and the wounds from that encounter are still tender. Now they must put aside their differences: to fight a greater evil, both Whitman and Sulky must come to terms with their past. In the end only one will survive this New Mexico showdown.

Cover design by Christopher Wait, High Pines Creative
Cover photograph © Getty Images / Thinkstock

U.S. Softcover

Visit Wheeler Publishing
online at gale.com/
wheeler
Visit our corporate website
at www.gale.com

ISBN-13: 978-1-4328-5595-6

9 781432 855956

Copyright © 1989 by Preston Lewis.
Wheeler Publishing, a part of Gale, a Cengage Company.

ALL RIGHTS RESERVED
Wheeler Publishing Large Print Western.
The text of this Large Print edition is unabridged.
Other aspects of the book may vary from the original edition.
Set in 16 pt. Plantin.

LIBRARY OF CONGRESS CIP DATA ON FILE.
CATALOGUING IN PUBLICATION FOR THIS BOOK
IS AVAILABLE FROM THE LIBRARY OF CONGRESS

ISBN-13: 978-1-4328-5595-6 (softcover)

Published in 2018 by arrangement with Preston Lewis

Printed in Mexico
1 2 3 4 5 6 7 22 21 20 19 18

NEW MEXICO SHOWDOWN

PRESTON LEWIS

WHEELER PUBLISHING
A part of Gale, a Cengage Company

GALE
A Cengage Company

Farmington Hills, Mich • San Francisco • New York • Waterville, Maine
Meriden, Conn • Mason, Ohio • Chicago

To Aunt Mildred,
for her sense of history,
her encouragement and her love